MANSON IN HELL

Manson in Hell

Greg Sterlace

BOOKS BY GREG STERLACE

Manson in Hell (2022)

Movies 365: A Good Movie for Everyday of the Year (2019)

Trump Unhinged (2017)

Bob Dylan: What the F*ck Happened? (2017)

The Beatles Album Guide: 1963-2016 (2016)

The Beatles: Having Read the Book (2015)

MOVIES DIRECTED BY GREG STERLACE

Manson in Hell (2022)

Catcher in the Rye with Diamonds (2018)

The Big Mess (2008)

Sweet Jesus (2006)

Failure (2004)

Ross & Gwen (2002)

DEDICATION

For Nicole Bermingham

And

Jill Jablonski

ACKNOWLEDGEMENTS

My beautiful wife Paula makes all things possible. Want to wear my Al Pacino *Scarface* silk shirt at our wedding ceremony? No problem. Want to make a movie about John Lennon's killer and the workings of his mind? No problem. Want to write a book about the 20th Century's most notorious cult leader and mass murderer? No problem.

...and I would be remiss if I also didn't mention super genius Lori Michaels, little Eugene Kelly of Los Angeles, California, and the four actors on the front cover of this book. From left to right we have Gweniviere Kiersz as Sharon Tate, Constance Caldwell as Susan Atkins, and Beth Kennedy as the embodiment of the Devil....and idiosyncratic vocal stylist John Blake as Charlie. You can see John as he tours the U.S.A. with his bands Green Schwinn and Red Huffy...and coming soon John will be starring in America's number one tribute act... Charlie Manson's Good Time Gospel Hour with the Manson Family and the Moron Tabernacle Choir.

HE WAS ONLY WAITING FOR THIS MOMENT TO ARRIVE

"...aware of the flat intellect of most mass killers, the extremists admire and are impressed with Manson's unquestioned intelligence, the offbeat and sometimes searing nature of his insights, his enigmatic answers and allusions, and a mental deftness that allows him to speak in riddles, always with an underlying message. In short, they are drawn to the mystery of Manson."

Vince Bugliosi (so called) 25th Anniversary Edition of *Helter Skelter*

The 9 Commandments of Charlie

I   Do as I say

II   Follow your love

III   Drink from the well

IV   Be where you are

V   Don't ever regret

VI   Give up your mind

VII   Forgive those you've wronged

VIII   Leave nature alone

IX   Wait for my sign

Charles Manson sits down for his first in depth interview since he died.

CHAPTER 1

THE AFTERLIFE

STERLACE: Thank you for talking to us, Charlie.

MANSON: Ain't got nothin' better to do.

STERLACE: Do you think you deserve to be here?

MANSON: They could of put me in heaven. I'm not so bad.

STERLACE: You got a bad rap?

MANSON: Shit, no matter what I do, they say Charlie's a bad man, Charlie's evil, Charlie's this, Charlie's that. Charlie should be in prison. Never wanted to leave prison. Begged them to leave me in prison.

STERLACE: Now you're in a different type of prison.

MANSON: Like I got some other choice. Like any of us got any other choice. You're always where you're meant to be otherwise you wouldn't be there.

STERLACE: So, you do think you belong here.

MANSON: I'm where I am and you're where you are and everybody in heaven and earth are where they are and sometime soon the word will end, and all the sinners everywhere will join me.

STERLACE: You think the world is going to end soon.

MANSON: It says so in the *Bible*. When the world gets so screwed up that people are worshipping false idols and raping the land and fighting unjust wars then Jesus is going to show back up and that's it, the end.

STERLACE: At one time you thought you were Jesus.

MANSON: I'm still trying to figure out who or what I am.

STERLACE: You're a killer.

MANSON: I have killed nobody nor ordered anybody to be killed.

STERLACE: That's hard to believe.

MANSON: I have my truth and you have your truth. If you already know something you don't have to talk to me about it. You can just talk to yourself.

STERLACE: So, you're innocent.

MANSON: I'm just saying I didn't do, I can't do, the things they say I did do. If I could do the things they said I did then I wouldn't have been in prison for forty years. I would have been out wandering the desert. I would have told the guards let me out and they would have let me out. They say I can control minds. Am I controlling your mind right now?

STERLACE: No, but...

MANSON: I'm not the messiah and I'm not the devil. I'm a teacher and I've been trying to get a message through to you and people like you for a long, long time but you won't listen. You never listen. You're like all of them that want to ask your silly questions about things you can never understand and take up my time with bullshit while you're eating creatures that are better than you and you're polluting the water and the air and chopping down our trees and making the bees go away and all the while you're playing stupid little games when you should be paying attention but you're too busy running around with your head in the sand watching your tv and listening to your radio and looking at your computer and talking in your phone when you should be noticing how everything is falling down around you and it ain't getting any better and it's not gonna get any better because you're all out for yourselves. You're not here for the planet. Mother Earth would take care of you if you let her but you don't care because all you care about is money and depleting our precious natural resources and stripping the land and spilling oil in the sea and all the evil corporations are holdin' hands with the government and you don't do anything about it. You just talk and talk and talk and go to your jobs and screw your wives and ignore your children. Don't look at me. Look at yourselves.

STERLACE: Do you think you could lead us?

MANSON: Would have guided you if you had let me but you put me in chains and threw me down the hole and stomped on my spirit. They talk about me controlling things, but I've been controlled all my life by teachers and preachers and doctors and cops. I've been in and out and up and down. I'm everywhere and everyone. I'm everything you want me to be and nothing at all. Now I'm dead so people think the show's over but it's just beginning. When you're dead you're not old anymore. You get your mind back, you get body back, but they take your soul and they blow it up and burn it down and it keeps going like that through all eternity. It's what has to be. It's what it is. It's what it was. There ain't no future and there ain't no past. You'll be with me soon. In fact, you're already here. Maybe they won't let you out after you've seen what you've seen.

STERLACE: And what's that?

MANSON: How it is down here, how it looks, how it feels, how it tastes, how it sounds. How it's all one long day. How the sun never comes up, how the moon never shines. Just darkness and sadness and frustration and despair.

STERLACE: It sure is a fascinating place.

MANSON: You think so, huh?

STERLACE: I do. After all those years waiting to get down here, does it match what you thought it was going to be?

MANSON: Well, it's not exactly the way I pictured it. It's not as warm as I thought. It's not as hard as I thought. I mean, my cell's not that small and they allow conjugal visits and I can see and hear and talk. It's not that bad. It's just you know those fuckers in heaven are having a better time feeling blissful and that kind of pisses me off, but I never really believed I was gonna make it there. Didn't think I had it in me. Just glad those goddamn atheists were wrong about it just being nothin'. Won't they be surprised?

STERLACE: Who do you have conjugal visits with?

MANSON: Whoever asks me. Men. Women. I never ask them. They always ask me. They want me to make love to them. I can take it or leave it. Mostly I take it. There's plenty of sex here. All kinds of different positions. Sometimes I organize the other sinners into groups of three or four or five. I feel it and I do it. Love is pain and hate is love. Could show you some things that would blow your mind. I miss the desert and the trees and the birds and the air. Want to talk to God. Like to talk to Him sometime. Sit Him down and find out what's what. Got a lot of questions.

STERLACE: Like what?

MANSON: Like why He did what He did. Why He's doing what He's doing. Why He's not watching over His children and His plants and His trees and the woods and the jungles and the sky and the monkeys. Like where did He come from and where is He going and where are we going and when are we going and why are we going and what are the answers and what are the questions and how did it happen and why did it happen. Was on the cross and I'm still on the cross and I'll probably always be on the cross. Can't get off the cross. There's no way out and there's no way in. I can't begin. I can't end. I'm here. I'm there. There's no right. There's no wrong. There's no beginning. There's no end. Why the moon and why the stars and why the sun? If I could save the world then I'd save the world. But I can't cause they don't want it. They don't see. They can't see. They don't want to see. They'll never see. You ask questions but you don't listen. You never listen. There's hell and there's heaven. Depending on what you done. There ain't no in between. There's a thousand million universes and you're in all of them and I'm in all of them. We all live and we all die. Then we live again. Unless it's your time to stop living. I ain't been told yet if this is the end. Will I live again? Will I die again? They ain't told me. I'm still waiting.

STERLACE: You found these things out since you got here?

MANSON: I found a lot of things out since I got here. I found out some things I didn't want to know.

STERLACE: Like what?

MANSON: Like what people are really thinking while they're smiling and they're nodding. They're thinking about how they hate you and they don't trust you, how you're nothing but dirt.

STERLACE: You do have quite a reputation.

MANSON: Didn't ask to be born. Didn't ask to die. You made me what I am. Didn't ask to be this way. Could have been a man in a suit going to work. Could have been a preacher in a church asking for your money. Could have been a famous singer singing my songs and healing the world. All I wanted to do was play my guitar. All I wanted to do was share my love with the world. But they wouldn't let me. If they had let me stay and play my guitar and sing my songs things would have been different.

STERLACE: So, you're blaming society?

MANSON: Well, it ain't my fault. Was made by your world. Didn't do nothing that I wasn't programmed to do. You take a man and you knock him down, bit by bit you chip away till there's nothing left and you ask him to be what you want him to be, to go against his nature, to say yes and please and thank you. You want us to comb our hair and say our prayers and believe what the president says. But the president lies, the government lies, the papers lie, the TV lies and we're supposed to swallow the lies and wait for more lies. They accuse me of murder but the government's killing people every day. Got troops deployed and they're dropping bombs and they're fucking up the planet and they won't stop.

STERLACE: So, I hear the devil is trying to rehabilitate you.

MANSON: Yeah, Beth's got her claws in me.

STERLACE: Beth?

MANSON: Yeah, Beth. That's the devil's name. Beth's teaching me that I had it all wrong. Beth's teaching me that I should love my brothers and sisters. Turns out, racism is bad – sexism is bad – hate is bad – violence against others is bad. Beth says when I learn all these things for real and take them into my heart I might have a chance someday to make it to heaven where I would get to hang with Jesus and The Father and The Spirit. But she says that in my case, it might take a long time, maybe a thousand years. But she will know when I've really grasped the Truth, grasped Goodness because she can read my mind. She knows exactly what's going on in there and it ain't pretty. Sometimes I think thoughts now just so she'll listen to me. But she knows I'm doing it on purpose. Beth will know when I'm cured and then I might have a chance to truly be saved. When Trump gets here I might be ready to be a mentor myself. He might take longer than me.

STERLACE: What's it like to die?

MANSON: Don't think somebody like you could understand. It's something you need to experience firsthand like making love.

STERLACE: Try me.

MANSON: It's a trip. You're living. You're getting older and older and dumber and dumber and number and number. You're drooling all over yourself and you're wondering when it's going to end. You ain't as sharp as you used to be. It's hard to stay on top of your thought. You struggle. It's harder to hear, it's harder to see, it's harder to move. You wonder what's going to happen. Then it happens.

STERLACE: What does?

MANSON: You think you're a fallin' asleep. But you're changing. All your memories are strolling past you kinda slow and you see your childhood and you see your mother going to the bedroom with your uncles and you see Howdy Doody on TV and you see George and Sadie and Tex and some strangers riding horses and you see Nixon and Agnew and you see all these girls dancing around a bonfire. The prison guards and the goddamn parole board are smiling at you and faces are staring at you as they walk you down the hall and they look like they want to kill you and the oceans are being poisoned and they're flying planes into buildings and they're killing the poor innocent creatures, going out a hunting and defiling the land and ripping apart Mother Earth with no thought for tomorrow and you're betrayed by those you thought loved you and you remember your dreams and you're a floating through time and space and the poor are going to rise up against the rich and take what's rightfully theirs.

STERLACE: And then?

MANSON: And then you're falling like a baby down a hole and doves are flying and you're crying and you go through the universe like a star and there are monsters everywhere and you don't know where you are or why this is happening and a man takes your hand and sparks fly and dogs howl and they drop you in a cell and put you in a prison. You fall asleep and you wake up and hard things feel soft and soft things feel hard and you're hungry and you're tired and they put you on a rack and stretch you out. Everything is gone and everything becomes and they're hosing you down and reading you the rules. No smoking and no drinking and definitely no thinking.

STERLACE: And that's what dying is like?

MANSON: For me. I can't rightly say what it'll be like for you because you're so busy with your questions, asking about things you'll never understand. Can tell you the truth about death and you nod your head, but you don't get it 'cause you're on a different plane. Could cure you but you don't want to be cured. You'd rather stay stuck right where you are, down in the hole with no clue about how to live right. Shit, somebody like you might not even understand how to live right when they're dead. You might need to live a thousand billion million more years before you see the light and even then you'll probably still be eating meat and killing bugs and wondering why you don't ever feel quite right.

STERLACE: I feel fine.

MANSON: Man, if you felt good you wouldn't be down here talking to me trying to find out what's what. You'd be off on your own all alone with your shit together. Why are you looking for answers? You should know by now that there ain't any questions. Everything been answered already. Can't tell you anything you don't already know.

STERLACE: Some people say that Death is the ultimate trip.

MANSON: Could be, reckon it could be. But what if there is something else after?

CHAPTER 2

RELIGION AND PSYCHOLOGY

STERLACE: Let me get your thoughts on the *Bible* starting with Noah's Ark.

MANSON: Somehow folks let it pass when God does something evil like killing off most everybody on the planet but when I make the slightest little mistake, they're all over me like the plague. Why should I be held to a higher standard than God almighty? It ain't fair. It was never fair. It'll never be fair. How He could kill off all those lovely creatures that He himself created is beyond me. Killing people that were not living up to His standards is one thing. They deserved it. But drowning all those innocent horses and giraffes and zebras, there was no call for that. Who does God think He is?

STERLACE: Adam and Eve.

MANSON: Well, he told them not to eat the Apple but they did anyway. But being thrown out of paradise ain't all bad. We might not have got the gift of music if that hadn't of happened. 'Course maybe we wouldn't have needed music to sooth our souls if we were still lolling around in paradise. So, it could go either way, like most anything.

STERLACE: The Crucifixion.

MANSON: Know what that's like. Ever since I was a baby they've been stringing me up on the cross, pounding nails into my hands and feet, whipping me and mistreating me. Don't deserve the abuse, not then and not now. Wish it would stop but there ain't no end in sight.

STERLACE: Are you the King of the Jews?

MANSON: I'm the King but not of the Jews.

STERLACE: Parting of the Red Sea.

MANSON: I thought I could part the Ocean but no matter how hard I tried it never happened. But maybe now that I'm here, maybe I've got special powers to cure the sick and feed the poor. Maybe being here is a gift from the Gods.

STERLACE: You mean God.

MANSON: I mean Gods. Ain't you familiar with the holy trinity? One and one and one is three. God ain't one. He's three. Any schoolboy knows that. God the father is on top of the throne. Coming next is his one and only son. He didn't have no daughters as far as I know. Then there's the Holy Ghost or Holy Spirit as I call Him. Believe He's the one who did the deed with Mary. Someone must have.

STERLACE: How do you reconcile people worshipping what they call the one true God, when he's really three?

MANSON: Sometimes no sense makes sense. Logic is not the only option. Where do the aliens come from? Who was God the father to God the father?

STERLACE: So, you do believe in aliens.

MANSON: Not a case of believing. Been on their ships many times. Been probed and prodded like you wouldn't believe. Been to Venus, been to Mars. Nice fellows, the aliens. 'Bout my size, 'bout my weight.

STERLACE: When was your first experience with them?

MANSON: 'Bout '47 I think it was. After the war. One night, sitting in a car I stole, minding my old goddamned business, when all of a sudden I'm lifted straight through the roof and flung up towards the moon. Didn't know quite what to make of it. Things like that made me grow up real quick.

STERLACE: And it happened again and again?

MANSON: Yeah. Whenever I was least expecting it there they'd be. At the foot of my bed or popping up out of the closet. Sometimes it would scare the bejeezus out of me. Sometimes I'd get real calm, look them in the eye, and tell them I ain't going. Not that that stopped them.

STERLACE: How would you fix religion?

MANSON: No one's God is better than anybody else's God. The Mormons ain't better than the Catholics. The Catholics ain't better than the Jews. We all flow into one stream. People would dig life differently if they could experience death first. When you go blind complain about the scenery.

STERLACE: Do you take the *Bible* as literal truth?

MANSON: Sure. God was doing a lot of interesting things those days like drownin' everybody and orderin' Abe to kill his son and kickin' Adam and Eve out of paradise and sending his only son to die for all. Though as far as I can tell Jesus ain't none the worse for the wear.

STERLACE: I understand you have your own set of rules that you like your disciples to follow.

MANSON: Yeah, the nine commandments of Charlie I like to call them.

STERLACE: How did you come up with them?

MANSON: Was looking for a way to get my thoughts out to all the good little boys and girls. So, I wrote some shit up off the top of my head and it *was* shit. Squeaky said you can do better than that and she was right. So, I rewrote the list and it came out much better.

STERLACE: Commandment I   Do as I say

MANSON: Well, that one says it all. Whatever I say goes. And don't laugh when I command you. Just follow my law to the letter and everything will be alright.

STERLACE: Commandment II   Follow your love

MANSON: I am your love and if you do what I say you won't get hurt because I am the truth and the way and the light. Whoever follows me will have everlasting bliss.

STERLACE: Commandment III   Drink from the well

MANSON: They call it the well for a reason because it makes you well when you drink from it. Don't suck up the dust, drink some cold water. I don't know of a man, woman, or child who doesn't like a nice drink, to quench their thirst.

STERLACE: Commandment IV   Be where you are

MANSON: Too many people would do anything to not be where they are right now. But they're still there whether they like it or not.

STERLACE: Commandment V   Don't ever regret

MANSON: You can't change the past so stop worrying about it you stupid little fool. This goes for the future too.

STERLACE: Commandment VI   Give up your mind

MANSON: Go with the flow. Stop analysing the fuck out of everything. If you're sitting, sit. If you're eating, eat.

STERLACE: Commandment VII   Forgive those you've wronged

MANSON: Even though they deserved it let them off the hook. Don't let them make you feel guilty. You didn't do nothing wrong. You did what you had to do.

STERLACE: Commandment VIII   Leave nature alone

MANSON: Leave Mother Nature alone shall be the whole of the law.

STERLACE: Commandment IX   Wait for my sign

MANSON: Always got a new message for you. So stay tuned, there's more to come.

STERLACE: What was your experience with Scientology like?

MANSON: A man came to me while I was a sleeping and woke me up and I said what the fuck man I was sleeping, and don't you know it's best to leave rabid dogs alone. Might be a little ferocious when they're awake. If I'm sleeping and some stupid motherfucker wakes me up in the middle of the night in the middle of one of my love making dreams or the one with the woman a hanging on the clock upside down and I'm tied to the mast and screaming in the wind with the force of a million billion sea urchins scavenging for food, then he might be in a bit of trouble whether he's looking for it or not. I don't care what a man does as long as he don't do it to me.

STERLACE: Can you remember about Scientology?

MANSON: They say your soul was born 75,000 years ago on another planet and the secret to life is knowing that and using that to get yourself clear. So, I did that but there was nowhere else to go once you got there but I'm still feeling clear to this day.

STERLACE: You sound a little murky on the details.

MANSON: I sat on a rock and I shared what I learned.

STERLACE: We'll come back to Scientology.

MANSON: I believe El Ron was a good man or a god man or a sailor or a sheep. Unless you walked in his shoes or Joe Smith's shoes, then it's hard to understand the love they shared with the rest of the world. Let me tell you something. It's coming back to me like the leopard comes back to the trees. I've been x'ed out of your world so many times. Now I'm in a different place, where the river flows red. If there's one thing I could show you that you would understand it is this.

STERLACE: You're not making any sense.

MANSON: Didn't ask you to come here. Not asking you to leave. You ask questions but you don't want the answers. You ever sing a song or pick a flower or drive a car or do a handstand or sail to sea or chop the wood or take off your clothes and look in the mirror and see something you don't like or force yourself to sit still and think for a minute about where you are and what it means and why it is and cry some tears and fight your wars and kill your sons and leave your daughters and wonder why they don't love you.

STERLACE: What's your personal philosophy?

MANSON: Do unto others before they do unto you.

STERLACE: What did you think of Bugliosi's last book? (*The Divinity of Doubt*)

MANSON: He got a lot of things wrong. That might be why he ended up here. Don't think for a second Saint Peter liked all that shit he was spouting about how there probably ain't any God and how if there was He wouldn't punish us sinners. He damn well does punish us sinners and I see now we deserve it. We took the wrong path out of the village and we should of turned back before it was too late.

STERLACE: Have you talked to him since you got here?

MANSON: God?

STERLACE: No, Bugliosi.

MANSON: Yeah, I talked to Vince. Had a nice little reunion. Thanked him for giving me life. He wanted to put me to death but they wouldn't let him. He was a bit perturbed you might say about ending up here. He said in his book that he didn't see what was so great about heaven, but you can damn well believe that he'd like to be there now. Stupid little fucker. Got what he deserved. He went around thinking he was better than me and everybody else, but it turns out he was like a lot of the rest of us. Just a mangy scraggly dog begging for dessert. Don't feel sorry for him. Why should I? Nobody feels sorry for me. He wanted to believe I was evil. That he did mankind a special service by keeping me out of their hair. But who's crying now?

STERLACE: I'll say a word and you say the first thing that pops in your head.

MANSON: Why?

STERLACE: It will help me figure you out.

MANSON: If I can't figure me out and a million trillion doctors couldn't figure me out how do you figure you're going to figure me out.

STERLACE: Just give it a shot.

MANSON: No.

STERLACE: Yes.

MANSON: No.

STERLACE: Now you're getting the hang of it. Let's try another. Father.

MANSON: Asshole.

STERLACE: Mother.

MANSON: Adjacent to asshole.

STERLACE: Drugs.

MANSON: What I'd like to be doing right now.

STERLACE: Garbage.

MANSON: You.

STERLACE: Pain.

MANSON: You. This ain't getting us nowhere.

STERLACE: Where do you want to get to?

MANSON: Don't want to get nowhere. Just want to be.

STERLACE: Mushroom.

MANSON: Cloud.

STERLACE: See, isn't this fun.

MANSON: Would enjoy myself more being roasted over an open pit with an apple in my mouth.

STERLACE: Let me show you some pictures and you tell me what you see.

MANSON: See an asshole trying to show me too many pictures. Can't you see that saying words at me don't do anything and showing me fuzzy pictures don't mean anything. Be straight with me and maybe I'll be straight with you.

STERLACE: Ok. Did you learn nothing from psychoanalysis?

MANSON: Learned that I was smarter than all the doctors with all their fancy degrees. Poked and prodded me to no avail. Couldn't help me, maybe because I was beyond help. Couldn't cure me because there's no cure for life. Well, of course there is and that's where I'm at now. Didn't ask to be here. Rather be somewhere else. But you're always where you're going to be. You might astral project across the world, might fly a flying carpet across the universe but you'll still end up where you started from. At one time there was nothing. Then there was something or maybe there was always something. Maybe I was always me since the planets were forming and the stars started shining. Was the moon always there or did it show up one day in the sky and freak everybody out? How did everything begin? Was God always around or was he born and if he was born who were his parents and weren't they Gods? Must have been it seems but who knows. Still waiting to talk to God to get the answers. But He hasn't shown himself to me...yet.

STERLACE: Maybe He's a woman.

MANSON: Maybe He is though if He was you wouldn't be calling Him He.

STERLACE: Did you ever want to be a woman?

MANSON: No, but it might be interesting. Some think we all got female and male crawling around in us and it just depends which one we want to be that day. Seen girls called bitches for the same behavior that you'd call a man strong for. Taught me down here that there's a double standard going on somewhere. Been called a male chauvinist but always thought women could do so-called men's work. Wouldn't have sent the girls out if I thought they couldn't do the job.

STERLACE: How did you settle on which girls?

MANSON: Looked for the ones with the most love in their heart. You gotta have a lot of love in your heart to help people the way they helped those people.

STERLACE: How is that helping?

MANSON: You're taking them out of the world and sending them right to heaven where everything is beautiful and there's no problems and no pain. That's a nice thing to do for anybody. Took Sharon beyond the valley of the dolls.

STERLACE: But even now you haven't seen heaven so you don't know that's true and anyways I'm sure they would have liked to live out their lives in peace.

MANSON: Haven't seen inside heaven but I seen the pearly gates and I can just imagine what's behind them. Gotta be a lot better than here.

STERLACE: Murder.

MANSON: What about it?

STERLACE: Just say the first thing that pops into your head.

MANSON: Told you I ain't playing your silly little game. It don't mean anything to say one word then another.

STERLACE: Of course it does.

MANSON: Not everything has meaning. Some things are meaningless. This thing you're trying to get me to do is meaningless. You could make up your own answers, interpret them any way you want and that would suit your needs just as well 'cause no matter what I say you're gonna decide what it means anyway. It's not what I say. It's what you choose to hear. You could say black and I could say white and you could say that means I'm a racist or that means I like zebras or that I see everything in black and white. But that don't mean it's true. You could say baby and I could say out with the bath water. You could say lonely and I could say towel. You could say rocket and I could say onion. But what would that prove? Nothing, really. You can find out more about me by asking me about me than with all your I'll say a word then you say a word nonsense.

STERLACE: Chair.

MANSON: Jesus H. Christ.

CHAPTER 3

MUSIC

STERLACE: Let's talk about your music.

MANSON: It comes through me like a bolt from the blue. Have to listen to it. Gotta get even with the ghosts and the demons and the spirits. People like me who dig music, who see music, who feel music, are different than people like you.

STERLACE: I feel music.

MANSON: I doubt it. I really doubt it. Don't feel it coming off you. Don't see your soul rising off you. So many folks lie to themselves. Are you one of them?

STERLACE: No.

MANSON: Think you are. You're one of those heathens looking for answers when there ain't any questions. Songs come to you, through you, around you, and you gotta grab them and hold them and shape them and breathe life into them. Songs are alive. But you're dead, all shriveled up inside, passing judgment on others you shouldn't be passing judgment on.

STERLACE: I'm not.

MANSON: You are. You sit there passing judgment on things you ain't seen. You ain't human. You're a question asking machine. Someday we'll rise up and take you down to the place you belong, to the place you deserve. You don't know what caring is. It's a ball of fire and it's coming for you. You can't outrun it. You can't undo it. It's in your heart, if you have any heart. Trying to get through to you but no one can. You're a nightmare and a nuisance. Goodbye to you now.

STERLACE: I just want to talk about your music.

MANSON: Then listen to it. Tell me what you hear. Do you hear angels and devils and little children crying for mercy? You're a sinner. That's what you are. I can see it in your empty eyes.

STERLACE: What was it like when you jammed with Neil Young?

MANSON: It wasn't jammin' exactly. We were at Dennis Wilson's house and I had a lot of great lyrics, a lot of great thoughts and Neil was digging what I was laying down. So, I spit out some words to him and he come up with some music and that was that. Unfortunately, he tried to sing along and that was throwing me off. I kept saying, "Shut the fuck up mother fucker, I'm trying to concentrate. Steve Stills might let you sing in Buffalo Springfield but I sing alone. Plus you're all out of tune, you sound like rats on a chalkboard." He stole a lot of stuff from me. "Southern Man," I came up with that idea. "Everybody Knows This is Nowhere" that was mine. Good old Mother Nature being on the Run, that was my concept. "The Needle and the Damage Done," that was me. Four dead in Ohio, seven dead in California.

STERLACE: What do you think of what the Beach Boys did to your song?

MANSON: They mangled it. They strangled the life out of it. They murdered it in cold blood and Dennis took all the credit for it. That's why I had to drown him later.

STERLACE: You had him drowned?

MANSON: I willed it. I was in my cell and I thought who should I kill today? Then later on I heard the news on the radio and I thought, good riddance. That will teach him not to steal my songs. He never stole another one after that.

STERLACE: If you had a band now and you were going out on tour what songs would you want to sing?

MANSON: Besides my own?

STERLACE: Yeah, like what songs would fit in your mouth?

MANSON: Probably "Sympathy for the Devil," "Another One Bites the Dust," "Paint it Black," "Devil in Disguise," "If I Only Had a Heart," "Tiptoe Through the Tulips," "Come on Get Happy," "Why Don't We Do it in the Road," and "The Addams Family theme song" repurposed to be sung about the Manson Family. They're creepy and they're kooky...

STERLACE: What would you open with?

MANSON: Well, there would be this bass playing and I'd come out all alone looking fine and dandy and sing, "Psycho Killer." That would wake them up.

STERLACE: And I don't have to guess what you'd do as an encore.

MANSON: Yeah, I would do "Helter Skelter." I'd go in the crowd and I'd get in their faces and I'd take them for a long ride in a dark woods to an abandoned house out in the desert where it's just me and them. I'd take them to a place that is higher than high and when we got to the bottom we'd come back to the top and we'd start all over again. It's been a long time bleeding. I always like to leave them wanting more. If you want music you'll get it from me just don't tell me what kind. I decide what music I'll make. If you want to hear songs you can listen to your phonograph. If you come with me I will give you an experience.

STERLACE: Speaking of that, did you ever see *American Idol*?

MANSON: Yeah, I saw that shit. Plastic people singing plastic songs to a plastic audience. Plastic judges judging plastic music for plastic America. Call in and vote. Vote for blowing the whole thing up.

CHAPTER 4

THE MIND

STERLACE: What's it like inside your mind?

MANSON: What's it like inside your mind? Is it a scary place to be? Do you wish you were someone else? Do you wish you could escape? Do you hate your mother? Do you hate your father? Do you hate yourself? Guessing you hate yourself.

STERLACE: I'm not asking about my mind. I'm asking about your mind.

MANSON: 'Cause you don't want to take a look at yourself. You're afraid of what you'd see.

STERLACE: I'm perfectly happy with myself.

MANSON: Yeah, I'm sure it was your dream to ask questions of people better than you. Have you ever been locked up and pushed down and thrown around? Have you ever had your freedom stripped from you? Just wanted to live out in the desert with my children and watch them grow.

STERLACE: What kind of father were you?

MANSON: The kind that laid down the law. Kids gotta have discipline, gotta be disciplined. Otherwise, they grow wild and get into bad trouble.

STERLACE: Is that what happened to you?

MANSON: My Ma didn't raise me right. She let me down. You might say she had me but I never had her. She had a lot of men and they all meant more than me and my father wasn't around. He was off God knows where. He didn't want me neither.

STERLACE: Do you think it would have helped you to have a more stable family life?

MANSON: It might have. It could have. I ain't sure. How can you know what would have happened if you had been born different? Didn't ask to be born into the world. Was kinda glad to leave it. There's a calm here. There's some light here. It ain't all bad. Not all the suicides end up here, not all the priests. It's sorta on a first come first served basis. 'Course I made it 'cause I was a very bad boy and they had to take me in.

STERLACE: So, what's it like inside your mind?

MANSON: It's black like the darkest night. Filled with laughter and sadness and magic. There's tall trees and cold water and heartbreak and unease. No one else could stand it in here. I can barely stand it in here. When I stop and think the sand sweeps over me and I'm drowning in disease.

I'm thinking and thinking, and I can't think any more. Not about you and not about your foolish questions.

STERLACE: Why do you think you're anti-social?

MANSON: How am I anti-social if I like rapping with folks? Explain to me how that's anti-social. Took in your children, the ones you didn't want, and I taught them and shaped them and molded them best I could. Would I do that if was anti-social? Wouldn't be talking to you if'n I was anti-social. I'd say get out of my face, leave me alone, bother somebody else.

STERLACE: We're getting off track again.

MANSON: Ain't never been on track. Was born into darkness and I'm still in darkness.

STERLACE: We're all just stuck in the moment, right?

MANSON: 'Course. That's all we have. Unfortunately, I'm spending this moment with you and your never-ending questions. Live for the moment, be in the moment, worship the moment 'cause you ain't got any other choice. The moment is a gift that's why they call it the present. Too bad, most of the time, it ain't what you want. You asked for a toy and they gave you some shit wrapped up in plastic and tied up in a ratty bow underneath your Christmas tree.

STERLACE: What's it like when you dream?

MANSON: Daydreams or night dreams?

STERLACE: Both.

MANSON: Well, they're different. They're awful different. Depends where you're at for daydreaming. In a cell I'd dream of being outside in the sun with girls laying next to me ready to do my bidding. Out in the sun I'd probably be thinking about what I was going to do that night, where I was going to go, what kind of car I'd steal, what kind of weapon I'd bring, what I was going to eat, what type of ice cream I'd slurp down, should I write a song, get some revenge, put my feet on a rock, pet a snake, maybe comb my hair. Night dreams are a whole different bag. Used to sleep like a baby 'cause my conscience was clear. Sometimes had dreams of being chased by a madman and that madman was me.

STERLACE: You get anything out of therapy?

MANSON: Like what?

STERLACE: Ideas on how to cope.

MANSON: Already know how to cope. All I do is cope. That's what we all do. No doc can see inside my head. If they could, they'd get out right quick. From the womb to the grave you gotta push through.

STERLACE: Do you have demons inside of you?

MANSON: Do now. They're crawling all around inside of me. Seems like whatever I did they wanna punish me for it. No trial and no forgiveness.

STERLACE: But when you were alive didn't you feel driven by demons?

MANSON: More like I drove myself.

STERLACE: Did you accomplish everything you wanted to accomplish?

MANSON: Don't think of it that way. What's a prisoner gonna accomplish? Just trying to stay alive from moment to moment hoping no one shoves a shiv in ya or burns your place to the ground. Tried to keep busy with my thought and my music. It's a high wire dive but they didn't put no water in the pool. If I could make you comprehend one thing it would be this.

STERLACE: What?

MANSON: All your striving for gold, all your striving for security don't get you anywhere. You'll still end up in a whorehouse overdosed and on your knees. Don't bother to repent. That ain't gonna help you at all. One way or another you're gonna get what you deserve.

CHAPTER 5

CRIME

STERLACE: Why do you think you became a criminal?

MANSON: Why did you become the kind of person you are? Not like I woke up one day and thought to myself how about being an outlaw who no one loves or wants or needs? Not like I thought to myself wouldn't I be better off spending all my time behind bars instead of being free like the rest of you. Didn't sit down and make a decision to fuck up my life. Didn't plan it out so I could get up close and personal to the penal experience full time firsthand. Wasn't like I was dying to only have sex with dirty disgusting men who would just as soon kill you as love you. Didn't want to leave my wife and all the other lovely ladies of the world. Missed them when I was in and when I got out for the last time I started collecting them like wild flowers. One after another I grabbed them off the vine and made sweet love to them but only if they asked me. They had to put in like an official request. Then I would satisfy all their needs and boy were they needy. Been called misogynistic but how could I be. Loved girls and they loved me. They gave up everything to be with me and I made them feel fulfilled and desired. If they were hung up on their father I'd tell them to pretend I was their old man. If they were hung up on their religion I'd tell them to imagine I was their priest. Had a system where I broke them down little by little by little piece by piece till it was just me and them. I'd be their mirror and they'd look at me and I'd look at them and we would become one and once we were one I'd introduce them to the wondrous pleasures of the orgy. Kind of orchestrate the girls for maximum effect. Dole out the acid and as we started to peak we'd really start to peak. Hands and mouths and arms and legs and shoulders and necks and lips and asses and feet and breasts and nipples and heads. Usually sprinkle in a few men for maximum effect like for seasoning. Way I'd get the men was to have the girls. Sometimes it'd go on all night, sometimes all day, sometimes the whole week, sometimes the whole month, sometimes it felt like the whole year. We'd be spinning through time and space. It'd be hot, then it be cold, then hot again. It was a giant ball of love and my idea was to try and all come together at the same time in one luscious swirling orgasm. Women and men screaming and moaning simultaneously. We would start slow and build slow and it was almost too much to take as the seconds became minutes and the minutes became hours and the hours became mornings and the mornings became evenings. We'd have music pounding away while we were pounding away and we were one happy family, one with each other hidden away from straight society and all its nasty hang ups and fears. When I had my cock in someone's body I felt at peace. Didn't matter if it was man or woman, young woman or old man, it felt right as rain as I tripped into the atmosphere into the stratosphere like a leopard messiah all was right all was locked in and locked tight. Was like taking the greatest drug while already ripping my head wide open on the greatest drug. Open my eyes and see three of everything, the music playing in my head and I could see the notes floating in the air. We came in colors and we became one with each other as dawn shattered across the sky. Lick me, suck me, kiss me I commanded my flock and it was delicious and delirious to make them part of something bigger than themselves. I was their father, their master and their Lord. Whoever came unto me would be blessed. Whoever gave of themselves would be rewarded. I was past insane. I was over the edge.

STERLACE: The question was: how did you become a criminal?

MANSON: Started small. Stole money out of my mother's purse, stole some of her jewelry. Then I hotwired cars for joy ride purposes. Then I'd sell the cars out of state to be more discrete, take the cash and buy a whore. Sometimes fall asleep in one of the cars and the cops would bust me. Did some pimping, some loan sharking, some armed robbery. Was a natural progression. Couldn't even imagine another kind of life. Shoot first and ask questions later. Crime and sex and drugs went hand in glove till they seemed intertwined in madness. If I could think of some way to rip off society I would execute it. I figured it was owed me. If I had a chance I'd drag a pig out in the woods and cut off his ear. One good thing about prison it gave me a chance to practice my guitar. Knew I was gonna be big someday, just didn't know how big.

STERLACE: You had a chip on your shoulder.

MANSON: You could say that. They say I was delusional, confrontational, irrational. What I was was institutionalized. Was a number, not a name. When they say jump, I'd jump. No way to live but it became the only way I knew. Got so used to the joint I didn't want to leave but they made me go. Begged them to let me stay. Asked for permission to go to San Fran and when I got there I saw Haight-Ashbury and Golden Gate park. Me and Mary and a couple of the girls were there when George Harrison showed up strumming his guitar and singing John's song about the Beautiful People. You can see Mary near George in one of the photos. Told George I played guitar too, but he didn't seem too interested. Kind of brushed me off. Could have taken him out right there but I loved him and I still kind of do. He was right. All things must pass. Kind of learned that the hard way. Me and Mary went to a couple parties at the Dead house and I met Pigpen and Jerry and the gang. Tried to get Janis and Grace to join me and Mary in the bedroom but they didn't fall for my tricks. Always regretted not ballin' both of them. How I would have loved to have made them sing.

STERLACE: What made you a criminal?

MANSON: You mean did I just one day decide to rob and steal and stab? You made me what I am. You forced my hand. All I wanted to do was lie in my bed all day and play my guitar. I'm a fawn in the forest and you've taken my life.

STERLACE: What did you think of Squeaky's attempt to assassinate Gerald Ford?

MANSON: Well, the key word there is "attempt." Like my girls to finish the job. Next time I hope she does.

STERLACE: Do you like death better than prison?

MANSON: Both are torture if you let it get to you. But I use my mind to control everything around me. Death don't get me down. I've given up on life many times.

STERLACE: How did you go about taking control of your followers?

MANSON: I'd look inside their souls and see what they wanted. Then I'd give it to them. If they wanted a daddy, if they wanted a friend, if they wanted a love, that's what I gave them. If they felt hate, I'd tell them that I understand. If they felt pain, I'd tell them that I understand. If they felt lonely, I'd tell them that I understand, and I did understand. They came to me. Didn't chase them down. I didn't choose them. They chose me. Took them in and gave them pride. I was their love. They were my children. Tried to help them grow. Gave them love. Gave them hope. That's what I gave them. That's what I had to offer. Didn't keep it for myself. I'm a selfish guy but I ain't that selfish.

STERLACE: Have you ever been in love?

MANSON: Been said that I'm in love with myself and maybe I am.

STERLACE: Why did you order the murders?

MANSON: Seemed like a good idea at the time.

STERLACE: That's it?

MANSON: That's it.

STERLACE: Simple as that?

MANSON: Simple as that. Don't question why I do things. Just do them. Betting you're the same way. You can ask the Lord to save you. You can cry until you're blue but you'll never be free till you realize this is all you got and it ain't gonna get any better. Going to get worse. You're gonna lose hope, you're gonna lose desire, you're gonna lose everything. No one's gonna care, no one's gonna sympathize. You were born alone, and you'll die alone.

Chapter 6

THE TRIAL

STERLACE: Do you think you were given a fair trial?

MANSON: Which time? Been on trial my whole life. Minute by minute, day by day. Brought witnesses against me, told lies about me. Made things up 'bout what I done. Exaggeration of the situation. Once was a handsome rodent who never did no one no harm. But they still cut off his ears, cut off his tail, and locked him in prison for life.

STERLACE: I'm talking about your murder trial.

MANSON: My murder trial? You mean the state's murder trial. Wanted to blame me for what the girls done. Wanted to say I was responsible. Admitted that I was back at the ranch on night one, admitted I was sippin' a milkshake at Denny's on night two. But they said Charlie was the joker behind it all. Whoever does the killing should do the time. Would you blame Jesus for what the Apostles done? Would you hold their master accountable for their sins? If life has taught us anything it's that the guilty will suffer at the hands of the innocent, the meek won't inherit the world, that all is unfair in love and war. Bugliosi was a master of language, a painter with words. Made a case out of thin air. Took away my freedom. Made me out to be a master manipulator, though in truth he was the master. Strung me up at the trial, screwed me over with the book, took me down a third time with the movie. Wish they'd let me play myself. Should have let me play myself. No one can really be me 'cept me.

STERLACE: How come you didn't take the stand?

MANSON: Truth be told I was scared of how Vince would twist my words, make me look bad. He made a lot of folks look bad and I didn't want to be added to the pile. Thought I might fold under intense interrogation. See now that I was a coward, but thought at the time I was protecting my ass. Shoulda done it, had the whole world's attention. But we can't change the past no matter how much we wanna. It's carved in stone.

STERLACE: Do you think it was a good idea to try and attack the judge?

MANSON: Look at it this way. If I attacked you for asking your stupid questions, would that be right? If it works out right, it was the right choice to do it. If it works out wrong, it was a terrible mistake. Made my point when I lunged for the judge. He knew who he was dealing with after that.

STERLACE: But it made you look guilty.

MANSON: Was already guilty. President Nixon said I was guilty and who knew more about being guilty than him?

STERLACE: So, you finally admit you were guilty of the murders.

MANSON: Guilty or innocent are just words. The fact that I'm where I am might give you a cosmic clue as to what the powers that be think. Jesus thinks I'm guilty. God the father thinks I'm guilty. The Holy Spirit thinks I'm guilty. For all I know the Virgin Mary thinks I'm guilty. Maybe I'm guilty and maybe I'm not. Who's to say?

CHAPTER 7

SONGS, BOOKS, AND SPORTS

STERLACE: Let's talk about your songwriting.

MANSON: Instead of murder, murder, murder?

STERLACE: How about starting with "Belly of the Beast?"

MANSON: That one is 'bout where I am now. Even mention in it that I'm spending time in the belly of Satan. Weren't no premonition. Knew for sure where I'd end up some day. This is a good one to listen to if you want to get a clear idea of what my time in prison was like. Everybody's against you. The warden, the chaplain, the guards, and the inmates. Fuck them all.

STERLACE: "Bet You Think I Care."

MANSON: Caring is the root of all evil. If you don't care you're better off.

STERLACE: "Cease to Exist."

MANSON: Thought my girl should give up her mind, her heart, her soul for me. The Wilson brothers ripped this song apart and used it for their own selfish purposes. Can't wait to meet Brian again.

STERLACE: "Winky Wonk."

MANSON: It's about my friend's son, he's a giraffe. Winky Wonk, already had a couple of kids, Audrey and Vivian, when I met him so he was an adult. My friend adopted him because he had an idea for a toilet for a giraffe that he wanted to test out, and then he found somewhere to adopt one. This all really did happen in actual life. Look it up on the internet. Winky Wonk's friend Peanut Butter is also a very inspirational giraffe. (sings) The heart of a giraffe is free/ You roam the plains so gracefully/ your eyes graze the mighty clouds/ I see your face and then I shout for Winky Wonk/ Winky Wonk with the heart of Africa on your side/ the soul of a giraffe is clean/ he roams the plains from sea to sea/ you reach up for his gentle power/ he opens up his eyes and so you shout for Winky Wonk

STERLACE: "No One Understands Me."

MANSON: Wrote that when I was 22 and the words still stand today. Still sums up my outlook. Hard to relate to you people. You're all so different from me.

(Sings) My mind's in torment/ so's my body/ Not having fun/ that's my hobby/ My bank account is fading quickly/ when I lend cash I'm charged a fee/ Please don't forget that I'm so impressed/ my glass is empty/ you're a mess. No one understands me/ I don't understand them/ No one understands me/ I'm glad I give a damn

STERLACE: "Devil Man."

MANSON: That was a premonition about me and my devil girl who turned out to be Beth. Beth, rhymes with death.

STERLACE: "Don't Do Anything Illegal."

MANSON: Gotta always make sure you have some ID with you because otherwise who are you, you're nobody. Kind of a joke for me of all people to preach against illegality.

STERLACE: "Rainbow Colored Happiness."

MANSON: I was really drunk in my basement with my friend Andy and we decided that there needed to be more songs about rainbows. (sings) Rainbow colored happiness and rainbow colored joy/ Rainbow colored happiness for every girl and boy/ come on everybody out there you've got to sing along/ because rainbow colored happiness is such a joyful song/ rainbow colored happiness rainbow colored joy/ rainbow colored happiness for every girl and boy/ We rode our bikes onto a cloud we're having so much fun so join us everyone.

STERLACE: "Ego."

MANSON: You gotta shove your ego in the back of your mind. Otherwise, things can get out of hand. My life's a good example of that.

STERLACE: "Go Downtown."

MANSON: (sings) Once they all were young and free/ They got eyes but they can't see/Go downtown/ go downtown/ Come on man on the bus on the bus/on the bus/ on the bus/ I'm living/I'm living/I'm living/I'm living/I'm living in hell.

Guess I foresaw where I'd end up when it was all over.

STERLACE: "Life is Death."

MANSON: That's what I used to think in prison and now that I'm in Hell I see that I was right. (sings) If life is death/ I must be in hell/ If life is deaf/ I can't hear the bells/ If life is death/ I must be giving/ If life is death/ this must be heaven

STERLACE: "I Never Took What I Gave to You."

MANSON: Never ask why but everything is the opposite of what it is. (Sings) I never walked the dog at night/ I never did the dishes right/ I never told you the real truth/ Deaf mute in a telephone booth/ I never felt as right as rain/ I never stopped all of that pain/ I never kissed her on the lips/ here come the boats, here come the ships/ I never watched *Mash* on Monday/ I never went to church on Sunday/ I never liked our big white house/ big Donald Duck or Mickey Mouse/ I never took what I gave to you

STERLACE: "Garbage Dump."

MANSON: With our garbage we could feed the world, if they only knew.

STERLACE: "I'll Never Say Never to Always."

MANSON: Like my own version of "I Forgot to Remember to Forget." Might be my most romantic song, my only romantic song.

STERLACE: "I Guess That Violence Means More Than Love."

MANSON: The world don't run on love.

STERLACE: "The Dead Don't Die."

MANSON: Now that I'm burning in eternal torment I kind of wish they did die. (Sings) The dead don't die/ They mate in the ground/ Then come back to haunt you

STERLACE: "Nihilistic Plasticism."

MANSON: Kind of like my personal philosophy. Used to sing this in the prison shower to some of my friends and lovers. (Sings) Sit on your ass and watch the world go by/ You don't care 'cause you don't try/ You eat meat/ You stuff your face/ You're one of those jerks from the human race/ I hate you all/ I wish you all were dead/ But don't let it go to your head/ I hang around hospitals to watch you suffer/ I don't care 'cause I'm tougher/ I don't sleep I stay awake/ Fuck you you're a fake/ I don't believe in wasting time/ there is no line for this rhyme.

STERLACE: "The Blind Association."

MANSON: (sings) No one can see/ not even me   Kind of feel like everybody's in the blind association. Everybody's got a blind fixation. No one can see what's right in front of them. They're blind to injustice, blind to terror at home and abroad. Turn off the news and switch to your favorite game show, talk show, law show, or cop show.

STERLACE: "Your Home is Where You're Happy."

MANSON: Home is where you get to be your real self, your true self.

STERLACE: "Alone in a Two Bed Room."

MANSON: That's about a PCP trip I went on outside some Frank Lloyd Wright mansion. Thought my friend who I was with was the Devil. (sings) Alone in a two bed room/ the mortgage has not been paid/ neither of them have been made/ the walls are closing in on me/ I shouldn't have done that PCP/ no I shouldn't have done that PCP/ alone in a two bed room/ there is something written on the walls/ it's yellow and it's very small/ it says pain yeah it says pain/ can someone shovel out the drive/ they say you're lucky to be alive/ yeah you're lucky to be alive/ alone in a two bed room/ there is someone pounding at my door/ thank god it's only the law/ they're taking me in for questioning/ they say that Coke is the real thing/ But how do I know Coke's the real thing/ maybe Coke is not the real thing/ stop telling me Coke's the real thing.

STERLACE: "We Live Together in our Car."

MANSON: Wrote that in the Haight sometime near the summer of love when I had just got some girls together. My flock you might say. We were like a family who had no place to go. They were all full at the inn. Was before we split for the desert to build something of our own. Don't remember the words too good but it brings back a pleasant memory.

STERLACE: "People Say I'm No Good."

MANSON: My personal favorite. Basically, people like you want me to be like you but I'm always myself and always will be even when I'm not… like when you say "I'm not myself today."

STERLACE: "I'm a Machine."

MANSON: Well, that one is 'bout how all us human beings are really machines. Eating machines, drinking machines, fucking machines, sleeping machines, bleeding machines. It's about living out in the desert in California ("It's a long hard road down to Mexico/ In a suit and a tie/ with a gun and sigh/ It's a long hard road/it's a long hard road") and 'bout how society tells you what to do and you gotta fight the urge to join in. ("Don't go to the show/ don't try to learn or know/drink your beer and glow/ turn off the radio, the radi, radi, radi, radi, radi, radi, radi, radio") Don't just be a machine. Think for yourself. It ain't against the law.

STERLACE: "Kill All the People that You See."

MANSON: My good friend Jim Morrison had some song 'bout tell all the people that you see to follow him and to get your guns and I thought that more applied to me. If anyone was gonna be followed around it was going to be me. As a kind of joke I used to sing it around the campfire as kill all the people that you see. Made more sense that way.

STERLACE: So, you were friends with Morrison?

MANSON: Yeah, we was tight for a while. Used to get as high as we could get together then go driving near the ocean. Had a lot of the same ideas. Both were singers. Both were poets. Went backstage at the Hollywood Bowl with some of the girls. Only time I met the other guys. Jim told me they didn't care much for me. Thought I gave off bad vibes. They were right.

STERLACE: How did you feel when he died?

MANSON: Kinda busy at the time with my own problems. He's down here somewhere I hear but I ain't ran into him.

STERLACE: What's your view on war?

MANSON: They'll tell you it's gotta happen sometimes to get all the bad blood out. But that's bullshit. Means old men sending young boys to die. Would never go to war. Like to pick my own fights. Better to kill who you wanna kill rather than complete strangers.

STERLACE: But weren't Tate and the LaBiancas complete strangers?

MANSON: Not complete. Talked to all three of them. Talked to Sharon at her door. Talked to the couple at their house.

STERLACE: Do you celebrate holidays?

MANSON: Never did see any need to make a big deal 'bout God's son rising from the dead, massacring the Indians, the new year beginning, or a baby being born in a manger. Have my own holidays. There's selfishness day, heartlessness day, and out of my fucking mind day.

STERLACE: Are you a sports fan?

MANSON: Yeah. There's nothing more exciting than watching a bunch of macho swine non-creative garbage wearing matching outfits as they chase a ball around a field.

STERLACE: So, what's your favorite?

MANSON: The one where they smack a human skull around with a stick.

STERLACE: What did you think of *Rosemary's Baby*?

MANSON: Tex and I saw that together. We dug it. Very realistic. Mia really went through hell in it.

STERLACE: Morgan Freeman mentions *Helter Skelter* in *Se7en*. Did you see that film?

MANSON: Yeah, that guy had quite a plan. I mean cutting off the cop's wife's head and sticking it in a box. You gotta give him credit.

STERLACE: Which drug is your favorite?

MANSON: Always partial to acid 'cause it took me places I ain't never been before. See beyond myself and tune in to the fact that everyone is me, that you're all extensions of my being. I am now and have always been the center of the universe. All roads lead to Charlie. When you're loving somebody, you're really loving me. Charlie sees you when you're sleeping. Charlie knows when you're awake. When you're alone in the middle of the night, I'm with you. When you're naked in the bathroom, I'm there beside you. When you're praying to your Lord, I'm receiving the messages.

STERLACE: What's the secret to happiness?

MANSON: You gotta realize there's a whole lotta water in the world and we only see the top of it.

STERLACE: How's that the secret to happiness?

MANSON: Oh, you want the secret to happiness?

STERLACE: If you don't mind.

MANSON: Don't mind at all, son. Always here to help.

STERLACE: So?

MANSON: So what?

STERLACE: Moving on. What's the best way to make new friends?

MANSON: Grab them by the throat until they notice you. Understand what they're telling you. Understand what you're seeing. Be their friend, don't ask them to be your friend. If they're racist, understand that. If they're sad, understand that. If they're feeling insecure, lonely, desperate, suicidal, dig that. If they got insomnia, mumps, measles, chicken pox do your best to cure them or stay away till they get better. Let 'em know you understand their wants and needs and feelings. They'll appreciate that. They'll feel you're on their side. That's when you got them. They used to say I was a manipulator but I could never manipulate anybody who didn't want to be manipulated. If you guide somebody to the promised land and they thank you for your service, you can't be in the wrong if all you did was right. Say somebody wants a cause to believe in, I might supply that for them. Say somebody needs to get to work, I might steal them a car. Say somebody needs a father, I might become their father. I'm different things to different people. To some I'm a god. To some I'm a lowlife. Actually, somewhere in between and aren't we all? Do you really think there's a person dead or alive who doesn't have a cross to bear, couldn't use a helping hand. If I had my way we'd be able to hear each other's thoughts and then it would all be out in the open. All of our love and all of our hate, all of our knowledge and all of our stupidity. People hold back 'cause they can hold back. What if it weren't so? We'd get honesty if we didn't have to talk but could let our thoughts do the talking. What we think in our minds is the truth. What we say, even what I'm saying right now, is partly truth, partly false, partly what we think the other person wants to hear, and partly what we really want to say. When others treat us bad, we want to push back with all our might but most of the time we just smile and nod and go about our day. Pride myself on my honesty but even I'm confused sometimes. Even I ain't perfect but I'm the best there ever was. If there's a person qualified to run the universe it's me. If I was in charge there wouldn't be no blizzards or hurricanes, no physical pain, no mental pain, no anguish, no fear, no regret. No tears would be shed, no grudges would be harbored.

STERLACE: "How to win friends and influence people" by Charles Manson?

MANSON: Yup, I ain't no Dale Carnegie but I'm the next best thing.

STERLACE: If you could do it all over again would you?

MANSON: Sure, 'cause I did it right the first time. Everything is clear in the rear-view mirror. When you're alive it's like being bounced around in a pinball machine. You're trying to catch a train but it keeps pulling out of the station. You leave the womb and you're never the same. No longer moist darkness but it's bright light all of the time. Neon lights and florescent lights, spot lights and stoplights. All the action just will not let up. You try to do the right thing but forces are beyond your control. But being dead ain't all it's cracked up to be either.

STERLACE: How come you never wrote your autobiography?

MANSON: It's all been said.

STERLACE: But not by you.

MANSON: Jesus never wrote a book. They wrote a book about him.   More of a thinker. Like thinkin' my thoughts then spewing 'em out loud. Get my point across that way. Never fails. Look into young folks' hearts and see their souls. Then I say what's what and they don't ask why. I'm the pied piper and I'm leading your children to salvation. So many people got their heads buried in books when they could be living.

STERLACE: Well, this is a book.

MANSON: True, but I ain't writing it. Can tell you all you want to know by just opening my mouth. Then again all those books about me not sure if they really capture me too well. Make me out to be some kind of nut. Really just a poor misunderstood boy who never meant anybody any harm. A good guy with a heart of gold. But they gotta sell their books and their papers and their magazines.

STERLACE: What happened to the Swastika on your forehead?

MANSON: Disappeared when they made me young again. Wouldn't mind having it back. Kind of miss it. Like an old friend gone before his time. Can read whatever you want into it. What's so beautiful 'bout it. Could be an Indian thing, could be a German thing.

STERLACE: You know and I know it's extremely offensive because of its association with the Nazis.

MANSON: Yeah, since I been here, I have been made to see it in that light. Might have been a mistake all those years. Certainly don't want to offend nobody. Been made to see there ain't necessarily good people on both sides.

STERLACE: What do you remember about your parole hearings?

MANSON: When I went they were fun, kinda like being on vacation. I would fuck around with those bastards...kind of like my TV interviews with less of those stupid questions interrupting my train of thought.

STERLACE: What was Geraldo Rivera like?

MANSON: Thought he was hot shit because he used to know John Lennon.

STERLACE: What was Tom Snyder like?

MANSON: Thought he was hot shit because he used to know John Lennon.

STERLACE: How about Charlie Rose?

MANSON: Has a good first name, doesn't have anything else good about him. He didn't pull that Harvey Weinstein open bathrobe stuff on me. Can't wait to sit down with all these assholes when they get here. Harvey, Charlie, Geraldo, Bill O'Reilly, Matt Lauer, Polanski, O.J., Fat Albert, Baretta...they should all be showing up shortly and I'll let them all know what's what. Beth's got a special place in her heart for these particular kinds of animals and she'll take good care of them the same way she has with me. They'll be punished right good before she teaches them how to be perfect dead souls.

STERLACE: Run into Michael Jackson down here?

MANSON: Yeah, sure. That son of a bitch is black again. The devil, she had me sleep with him for a while, kind of teach him a lesson. He'll think twice before he does any more babysitting.

STERLACE: How about Phil Spector?

MANSON: Instant Karma got him good. Gonna have him produce my next record. Charlie Manson's Good Time Gospel Hour with the Manson Family and the Moron Tabernacle Choir...featuring the hit single "Slashing Through to You with Love in My Heart."

STERLACE: You get mentioned fairly regularly on Stephen Colbert, Seth Meyers, and Jimmy Kimmel. They use you to make all kinds of salient points. On Tuesday August 2nd 2022 Colbert said in his monologue that you can't be too insane to run for office in the MAGA Republican Party. Colbert said it would be like being too crazy to join the Manson Family.

MANSON: Well, I'm a household name so it's easy for them to make their stupid little jokes using me as a punchline. They think they're funny but I don't see nothing funny about them.

STERLACE: Larry David said he'd rather golf with a fast Manson than a slow Funkhouser.

MANSON: When he gets down here, I'll curb his enthusiasm.

STERLACE: In *Thank You for Smoking* Aaron Eckhart says Michael Jordan plays ball and Charles Manson kills people.

MANSON: Don't he know that I take care of my business by proxy?

STERLACE: Adam Carolla said you had it made and you threw it all away.

MANSON: He may be right. If I had just stayed out of society's way, I could have stayed free to my dying day. Instead of being cooped up like a rat in a manger.

STERLACE: David Chase calls Mafia guys' sinister eyes Manson Lamps.

MANSON: I just call my eyes pretty.

STERLACE: Chuck Klosterman says the most bizarre film he could imagine is a documentary about your music career directed by Roman Polanski.

MANSON: When he shows up here soon maybe I'll sit him down and discuss that very project with him.

STERLACE: Let's discuss some of the many books about you. How about *Chaos*?

MANSON: Guy came up with some crazy idea that the C.I.A. was behind the murders. It was either them or the F.B.I. or B.B. King or Doris Day. Bullshit. Could just as easily say it was the A.C.L.U. or the S.P.C.A.

STERLACE: What about *Manson: The Life and Times of Charles Manson*?

MANSON: That was just a way to rewrite and resell *Helter Skelter* without giving any of the money or credit to Bugliosi.

STERLACE: How about *The Family* by Ed Sanders?

MANSON: That had some truth in it, some lies, just like all versions of my story. I'm the only one who could tell it straight but I never do.

STERLACE: How did it feel to be on the cover of *Rolling Stone* and *Life*?

MANSON: Like being the center of attention. Like people looking at me. Special even if my mother never told me so. Just another way to get my words out to the people. They were right to put me on there. Right to make me the *Rolling Stone* interview. For some reason, Hef never made me the *Playboy* interview. Could have run mine in the same issue with Polanski's. Hell, they talked to him more about me than 'bout his movies. Nice to be sent to the houses of all the mothers and their children. Wish I sold as many records as I sold magazines.

CHAPTER 8

THE BEATLES

STERLACE: How did your whole obsession with the Beatles double album begin?

MANSON: Well, I'd known for a year or so that they'd started sending me personal messages through their songs. Every time I'd listen, I'd hear something directed right straight at me.

STERLACE: For example.

MANSON: "Blue Jay Way" was about George waiting very impatiently for his friend to show up in L.A. and I had just left San Fran where I had met George who that very day was singing John's song about the Beautiful People which was what I called Mary and me and the other girls. Then George goes back to England and writes a song about waiting for his new friend in L.A. and when I get to L.A. the first thing I see is the Capitol building and the second thing I see is a copy of the new album on Capitol records with "Blue Jay Way" on it and I send Mary into Tower to lift it and she brings it to me and I magically decide to put the needle down on a random spot and what do I immediately hear but George singing about waiting for me to show up in L.A. He couldn't keep waiting for me so he must have went back and told the other Beatles how he had met me, how I was a groovy cat who was tuned into their rhythm and they must have decided right then and there to put a whole lot of songs to me on their next album which is what they did. I checked the lyrics to the show songs just to make sure I was hearing it right and I was right. It was all there in black print on a white backing which obviously was a clue to the upcoming black and white war. Then I looked at the photos in the album and it's as if they were speaking right to me. All these weird photos of Paul. Paul wearing a black carnation on his white suit and Paul with his shoes off and blood splattered on his feet and Paul in front of a sign saying I was you which I took to mean that he was me and I was him and we were all together and there was that weird photo of John with a big mustache in front of a sign that said the best way to go is by M.D.C. and I didn't think much of it at the time but we all know how that turned out and it wasn't pretty.

STERLACE: You know this all sounds crazy, right?

MANSON: It ain't crazy. It's just what happened. So, 1968 rolled around and I was waiting for them to give me the word. So I heard Paul sing you were made to go out and get her and I kept that in the back of my head and when I'd seen in the paper that we took out Sharon Tate kind of accidental like, I knew Paul had directed us to go out and get her. Meanwhile John was on the flip side singing that you could count him out on destruction so we bided our time and by the time the White Album had come out John had changed his mind about destruction and he was all in on it.

STERLACE: Don't you know he actually recorded the 'in' version first (during May and June of 1968) and the 'out' version second (during July of 1968) and issued them in backwards order?

MANSON: Bullshit. I heard him say out in the summer and in during the fall and it was obviously a sign to me that now was the time for Helter Skelter. The White Album had all the clues I needed.

STERLACE: You know the album was called *The Beatles*, right? There's really no such thing as the White Album.

MANSON: Bullshit. It's called the White Album. Wouldn't the fact that it's an album with a white cover be some kind of fucking clue? It was painfully obvious it was called the White Album because that's what I called it the minute I laid eyes on it. We heard it was out just in time for Christmas so me and Sadie got in the car and went to Tower and I told Sadie to fall down on the floor screaming so I could stick a couple in my big winter coat. Always say why pay for something when you can pluck it for free. So, I boosted them and took them back with us and I gave one to the girls to play and I took the other one to study. Knew this was it, their gift to me. The front cover was white, and the back cover was white. It was white all over just like whitey wanted society to be, but it was too late. The black man was rising up despite the fact or maybe because of the fact that their leaders kept getting gunned down. I ripped off the shrink wrap and opened it up and lo and behold there were our leaders in black and white. Just by looking at their sad faces I knew I was in for some very serious shit.

STERLACE: Did every song speak to you?

MANSON: No, not all. Most did, but you had to know how to read between the lines. They couldn't be too obvious because straight society might get wind of what they were laying down.

STERLACE: What's the first song that caught your ear?

MANSON: Had to be "Dear Prudence." Somehow the Beatles knew Mary had had a child and I had named her Prudence. Didn't know if I was the father because we were all screwing each other left and right and it was impossible to know who had knocked up who, but Mary said I was the father and that was good enough for me. Every day since Prudence was born, I had sung her awake in the morning. Used to always tell her how beautiful she was. It was like they were reading my mind. We were completely in tune.

STERLACE: How about "Glass Onion?" Didn't that one have a lot of clues in it?

MANSON: Sure did, son. Every line was pregnant. You could tell John was speaking directly to me and it was like going over everybody else's heads. He was talking again about Strawberry Fields, letting me know that no one else was in our tree, that there was nothing to get hung up about. There was no right and no wrong. We were all doing what we were supposed to be doing. We all were where we were supposed to be. Everything was love. Love was everything. When I ate an apple that was love. When I drank some milk that was love. When I stood on top of the mountain and looked down upon the sea that was love. John was singing about a place our family could go where everything flowed. We were always looking for it. It was where the other half were supposed to be, and we were the other half. I was the fool on the hill, and I thought sometime soon they'd join us there.

STERLACE: How about "The Continuing Story of Bungalow Bill?"

MANSON: I was Bungalow Bill, living in my bungalow at the ranch. I was Bungalow Bill and John was asking me what I had killed and wasn't it about time? I was getting a lot of direct messages. I knew I had to act on them.

STERLACE: "Happiness is a Warm Gun."

MANSON: Well, I used to think that was true. That's about shooting your gun during sex and shooting another person when they get in your way. Liked doing both.

STERLACE: "Blackbird."

MANSON: 'Bout the black man rising up against whitey and taking what was rightfully his.

STERLACE: "Piggies."

MANSON: The boys in blue were pigs and the rich fat cats like Roman and Sharon and the LaBiancas were pigs and they had to be taken out by somebody. What they needed was a damn good whacking. Tex and the girls scrawled piggies on the wall in blood. I thought the cops would blame the black man and the whites would start killing the blacks and it would be a bloodbath.

STERLACE: Why?

MANSON: Why what?

STERLACE: Why did you think a race war would ensue?

MANSON: Don't know. It made sense at the time. When it didn't happen, I was very surprised.

STERLACE: "Sexy Sadie."

MANSON: Well, that was mighty peculiar. I had re-named Susan earlier that year and I had christened her Sadie. More proof that me and the Beatles were on the same wavelength. When she started singing to the authorities 'bout the murders she made a fool of everyone. She'll get hers yet. In fact, she already has. Been spending a lotta time with her down here trying to make her see the errors of her ways

STERLACE: "Revolution 9."

MANSON: That was like a blueprint for what was to come. They were speaking my language. They were telling the black man to rise. On August 9 in the year 9 the police were first made aware of what was going down, what was coming down around their heads. The revolution had begun.

STERLACE: "Helter Skelter."

MANSON: I could dig what Paul was singing. The time had come for Helter Skelter.

STERLACE: But wasn't it just a song about a children's slide in a playground?

MANSON: That's what they want you to think.

STERLACE: What did you make of *National Lampoon* naming you the fifth Beatle?

MANSON: That's right on. Always how I thought of myself. Actually, come to think of it, I'm more important than Starr. I definitely write better than him, sing better than him. Maybe I'm the fourth Beatle.

STERLACE: When did you first hear the Beatles?

MANSON: Heard them on the radio. I get high. I get high. I get high. Like four angels in a choir sending messages of love. Always telling it like it is, like it'll be. Came down from above and showed everybody the light. Touched me like no one else. I could of become like them if they gave me a chance. You hear what you want to hear. I hear the truth.

STERLACE: And what is the truth?

MANSON: The truth is they were talking to me, sending me the word, and the word was love. Don't kill animals. Don't hurt what's better than you. Everything is love. Everything is right. If you think it you can do it. Like stepping out of one car into another. Singing in the day and singing in the night. We've lost our way. But we'll find it.

STERLACE: What specific messages were they sending you?

MANSON: Rise. Swim across the Atlantic. Join them in their yellow submarine. Kill some piggies. A lot of what they were saying was right on.

STERLACE: How did it feel to have John Lennon talk about you?

MANSON: What he say?

STERLACE: That you were balmy. That you were an extreme manifestation of those Beatlemaniacs who thought they were singing right to them. That you were made by the state.

MANSON: Yeah, I was x'ed out of your world by the cops and the judges and the wardens and the shrinks. They say I'm famous but what's that mean? That people know me, but I don't know them. I know them. I know everyone. When you lock your doors at night I slip in and stand at the foot of your bed. Could burn you any time I want and maybe I will.

STERLACE: Did you really think "Helter Skelter" was about starting a race war? Do you really think Paul McCartney would write a song about that?

MANSON: He denies it but that only makes it more true. If you listen to his voice, you'll hear him saying take those mothers out, take them out now. Where it ends, you'll never know.

STERLACE: Did John Lennon's murder affect you at all?

MANSON: People die every day. But if it's someone so-called famous then the TV and the papers make a big deal of it. It's no big deal. It just is.

STERLACE: What about George Harrison being stabbed nearly to death by an intruder in his house? Does that remind you of anything?

MANSON: It reminds me that we all got to go sometime.

STERLACE: I heard a rumor that at one time you thought "Dear Prudence" was about you.

MANSON: That's true. Works on multiple cosmic levels.

STERLACE: Actually, it's about Mia Farrow's sister.

MANSON: Why would they write about Mia Farrow's sister, she's nobody. They wrote it about me. They were telling me to come out and play. They was telling me to come out and announce my presence with authority.

STERLACE: So, John Lennon was over in England writing songs about you, a person he didn't know, a person he never met?

MANSON: That's right. Lennon wrote a lot of songs about me. Did you know I'm the walrus? I was sending him vibes across the Atlantic and Lennon was picking them up and sending me messages through his songs. Non-creative garbage like you wouldn't understand.

STERLACE: I guess not. How about "I Want to Hold Your Hand?"

MANSON: That was the first one I heard. I was sitting in prison, minding my own business listening to the radio. It was all that mindless top 40 junk that they used to spew out to a captive audience and all of a sudden I heard these guys singing about getting high. I get high, I get high, I get high...

STERLACE: They are actually saying "I can't hide..."

MANSON: No, they're not. I listened to it very closely, over and over, and I know they were trying to turn me on.

STERLACE: It's a love song.

MANSON: No, it's not. It's a drug song. Someone like you who has never been drugged out and left for dead in a corner can't dig the truth.

STERLACE: Of course not. I'm non-creative garbage. What about "Mother Nature's Son?"

MANSON: That was about me. I'm mother nature's son. All day long I would sit singing songs for everyone.

STERLACE: They seem to have written an inordinate number of songs about you.

MANSON: That's right. Even later on they were thinking about me. What do you think "Band on the Run" is about? I was stuck inside four walls, sent inside forever, never seeing anybody nice again...just nosey people like you. Could give you the answers but I don't want to.

STERLACE: What about "Ob-la-di, Ob-la-da?"

MANSON: Well if you want some fun...take it. Obviously, it's about a guy who is really a girl and keeps his face in a jar by the door. The Beatles were way ahead of everybody on this whole trans thing. They could see the future. Don't know how but they could. They were like four or five magicians up there in the clouds.

STERLACE: "Mind Games."

MANSON: Well, that's what life and death are all about. It's all in the mind. If you think you're happy then you are. If you think you are sad then you are. All you got is the moment and you can make of it what you will though it might be a little harder if you're up on the cross and the blood is draining from your body. But even then if crucifixion is inevitable try to relax and enjoy the ride.

STERLACE: Good advice. "Maxwell's Silver Hammer."

MANSON: Might as well be called "Charlie's Silver Hammer." Feel like Rose and Valerie were screaming from the gallery that Charlie must go free. This track is where I got the bright idea to attack Judge Older. Almost worked too. Charlie's silver hammer nearly came down upon his head. I'd still cut off his noggin in the name of Christian justice but I can't get anywhere near him. He's up in heaven with the judge of us all.

STERLACE: "Think for Yourself."

MANSON: Don't agree with this one. If you were really smart you'd have me do your thinking for you.

STERLACE: "I'm Happy Just to Dance with You."

MANSON: Don't buy this one. I was never happy just to dance with them. Always wanted a little bit more.

STERLACE: "Tomorrow Never Knows."

MANSON: Used to trance off into the Alpha listening to this one, float on a river for ever and ever. They say you can play the game of existence until the end, but it never ends. It just keeps going and going until they tell you to get off and even then it's not over it's just beginning.

STERLACE: "Honey Pie."

MANSON: This is the one where McCartney was telling me to record my songs so he could find me. Maybe if I got my songs out I would have ended up on Apple like James Taylor and the Hare Krishna singers.

STERLACE: "Eleanor Rigby."

MANSON: Well, I'll tell you where all the lonely people belong. They belong with me. Then I can teach them and I can guide them and I can show them the way.

STERLACE: "With a Little Help from My Friends."

MANSON: That's exactly how I lived my life. How I took care of the things that needed to be taken care of. Even when I was in prison for life I got lots of cards and letters from people who wanted to be my friends, who wanted to help me out. If I'd gotten probation I could have had the biggest family in the world. Maybe I would have started Manson town and served them golden Kool Aid.

STERLACE: "Run for Your Life."

MANSON: This one is about being jealous. But I was never jealous because all of my girls loved me and only me.

STERLACE: "All You Need is Love."

MANSON: Nothing you can do is wrong. Nothing you can do is right. It's just what it is. How can you be at the wrong place at the wrong time? You're always in the right place at the right time.

STERLACE: "Got to Get You into my Life."

MANSON: It's about taking drugs and letting them take you on a ride to the dark side to the light side to the right side. Maybe if some of these uptight right wingers took the right drugs they might see the errors of their ways. But that is not going to happen. That's never going to happen. They are just like the left wingers trapped in their own little bubble.

STERLACE: "Nowhere Man."

MANSON: That was about me. John wrote that specifically about me. He was sitting down one day trying to be clever, trying to write a clever song when my spirit came through him and he was moved and he wrote about me. About how I was nowhere, breathing the fumes of prison.

STERLACE: "Sun King."

MANSON: That's about me. When I was out in the desert I was the Sun King leading my people to the promised land of milk and honey.

STERLACE: "Mean Mr. Mustard."

MANSON: That's about me. Isn't it obvious?

STERLACE: "Lovely Rita."

MANSON: That's not about me.

STERLACE: In McCartney's new book on his lyrics he says "Apparently, Manson read hell into "Helter Skelter.""

MANSON: Nice to hear Paul is still thinking about me.

STERLACE: Why do you think Chapman shot Lennon?

MANSON: Well, after listening to those songs on the White Album and that song on *Mind Games* about do it, do it, do it now he probably felt like it was a good idea. Chapman was so crazy that he thought the Beatles were sending him messages in their songs. Chapman was so fucking crazy he couldn't follow the rules.

STERLACE: That sounds like your M.O. Isn't it possible, isn't it likely that John Lennon was just writing songs that had nothing to do with you or Mark? Nothing to do with you two at all?

MANSON: Well, he might not have been sending love letters to Chapman but he sure was to me.

CHAPTER 9

THE MURDERS

STERLACE: When did it first occur to you that it was okay to murder innocent people?

MANSON: I have killed no one nor ordered anyone to be killed.

STERLACE: Why not level with us? You're already being punished for your crimes against humanity.

MANSON: What about what the world did to me? What about all those times I put out my hand and you slapped it down? Just wanted to sing my songs and share my love but nobody wanted to help. Reached out and I gave out and I got slapped down and pushed around. Dennis didn't help me. Terry didn't help me. But I helped them. Gave them my girls. Gave them my love. Gave them my music. But that wasn't good enough for them. Oh no, that wasn't good enough for them. They said one thing and they meant another. They said we'll help you, we like you, we love you. But they didn't love me. They loved their money, and their cars, and their sweet easy lives. I was out in the desert climbing on that cross, picking fruit and berries, looking for the entrance to the promised land. We was going to go down and wait out the war and come back above when it was over. Wanted to take control. But they wouldn't let me.

The man didn't want to represent me. The man resented me for who I was and what I looked like and what I did. Hated me for who I was. Had to give them a sign so I gathered my friends and I gave them a plan and they carried it out and then the world knew who I was. They damn well sure knew who I was. If you cut down a tree, it don't grow back.

STERLACE: So, you admit you ordered the murders.

MANSON: I don't admit nothin'. I should be in heaven with all the other good little boys and girls. ONE, TWO, THREE, FOUR, FIVE, SIX, SEVEN. ALL GOOD CHILDREN GO TO HEAVEN. The shit is coming down now. Helter Skelter is coming down now. It's coming down on your head. It's time for judgment day and you'll be judged for your crimes. All you with your suits and your ties and your endless lies. You'll get what you deserve.

STERLACE: Why not come clean for the record?

MANSON: If I told you I ordered those people to be killed it wouldn't change anything. Once something is done it can't be undone. We can't go back to '69. There's no way to do it.

STERLACE: I'm not asking you to go back. I'm asking you to admit what you did.

MANSON: Ok. I did it. I admit it. Now, how long do I have to carry this cross?

STERLACE: Do you feel like society is going downhill?

MANSON: It's all been going south since Adam and Eve. If you ain't in paradise then you gotta get used to suffering and pain, eating shit you don't want to eat, taking shit you don't want to take. Society is phony smiles, weak handshakes, businessmen minding their own business and their business is how best to go about cutting their customers throats. They'll tell you that you can fit in, be one of the Beautiful People, get an erection when you ain't been able to get an erection in God knows how long. It's all a bunch of bullshit. The snow is melting, things are heating up. They claim we're more connected than ever but we're really more disconnected. Like to think I've brought people together. They all hate ol' Charlie. Wouldn't want your sister to marry Charlie, wouldn't want Charlie to babysit, oh no we'll find somebody else, don't leave him with our kids he might corrupt them, might teach them the truth. We don't want none of that. We want to program them, so they'll be good little boys and girls saying the pledge of allegiance, learning lies about Columbus and George Washington and Thomas Jefferson. Get them ready for a lifetime in a cubicle before being transferred to a more permanent box. No one tells them when they're young that life has no meaning, that you don't have to think, that there are no rules. You can't be whatever you want to be but you might be able to work a horrible job that you hate for low wages where you gotta answer to some jerk off boss who don't care about your problems 'cause they got problems of their own. The wonder is that you don't see more folks flinging themselves off skyscrapers when the working day is done. America was never great 'less you think evil politicians or slavery or burning crosses or prostitution or police brutality are great. Over two hundred years of genocide, homicide, suicide, and pesticides and they wonder why they can't look at themselves in the mirror and find anything there.

STERLACE: So, there's no hope.

MANSON: There's never been any hope. Folks are selfish and petty. They're out for themselves and nobody else.

STERLACE: If you were in charge how would you fix all our problems? Immigration, for instance?

MANSON: I'd say give me your tired, your poor, your lowlifes, your priests. Give me your deranged, your forlorn, your drunken masses burning to be free. Throw the borders wide open. Why are people so afraid? Probably 'cause they're scared little animals trying desperately to fit in. For Christ's sake Superman was an alien. The ultimate symbol of America was not only not one of us, he wasn't even from around here. Not only was he not American, he wasn't even from planet earth. Yet, you can bet all those bible thumping flag humping mouth breeders from God's country would embrace him with open arms 'cause they see he's white. But he's an alien, he's a goddamn illegal alien.

STERLACE: Death seems to have changed you.

MANSON: Well, what's the point of death if it doesn't change you? I've seen the light, I've seen the light, Lord hallelujah I've seen the light. It turns out that when you're alive you're worrying all the time about what you gotta do and who you gotta do it to. Here you can relax and think about some of those things you didn't have time for. Was programmed by my mother and my uncles, by my family, by society. Made me what I am but now I see differently. A lot of what I thought was wrong. Black and white are the same, men and women are the same, love and hate aren't the same. I was taught by your teachers, by your government, by your prison. But I was grown up wrong. Now I really see what is right, what is wrong, and what is justice. It's justice that I'm here but I still resent it. Couldn't see little by little what you were doing to me.

STERLACE: Take us back to 1968.

MANSON: We was living in the Yellow Submarine, but I felt confined like I wanted more space in a nicer neighborhood like a lotta people do. So, we ended up at Dennis' house 'cause I dug what they were doing and I hoped they'd record one of my songs and put it on a record and make a million for me overnight. So, he took us in, and the girls rolled joints and baked cookies and we played house until he kicked us out 'cause he couldn't stand all that happiness. So, we took off for Death Valley right around the time when that album came out, the one where the Beatles were singing songs directly to me. I could hear things that other people couldn't hear. Even when I was a kid, I could see things that other people couldn't see. Always had such a good time combing my hair in the mirror 'cause I would kind of trance out into the Alpha and realize we're all one with the universe. There's no stereo separation. Could be on top of a mountain or in the back bedroom and it was all the same thing. Didn't know when I was gonna die, how long it was gonna take but knew it would be relatively soon all things being relevant. What folks could never understand was we were all together and we would all go down together, and that I would have to be the one that would have to get things started. Helter Skelter was coming down fast and it would soon be upon us. We was going to make it seem like the blacks were killing the whites and there would be riots in the streets and the white man would turn on the black man even more than he already had, which is saying something. There would be a war with blacks on one side and whites on the other. No need for uniforms, your skin color would do. We'd wait it out in the land of milk and money that was just below the surface if we could only find the entrance. We never did. Seems a little crazy looking back but at the time I thought we were doing the only thing we could do, like it was fate, like it was what God wanted us to do. Don't really know if He really wanted it but I wanted it and that was more than sufficient.

STERLACE: What happened on Friday August 8th, 1969?

MANSON: I told Tex and Sadie and Linda and Katie to get a change of clothing and a gun and a rope and some knives because now was the time for Helter Skelter. They did what

I said like they always did 'cause I was their father and teacher and brother and they knew I always had their best interests at heart. Cared for them like they were my own children and like all children they needed guidance from above. Said go to Terry's house and kill whoever you find there. We were gonna send a message to the establishment, make ourselves heard. Told them show no mercy 'cause when had the pigs ever shown us mercy? You gotta understand it was a turbulent time and emotions were running high. Not so sure I was right now but back then I was positive I was doing the right thing, the good thing. You could say the righteous thing. Stayed at the ranch and they left in the car and the next day it was all over the papers and I knew it was time for phase two. So, I went with them to this neighborhood we used to hang out in and this time we brought Leslie and I went in and tied up this nice couple nice and gentle and told them no one was gonna hurt them. Didn't want them to start screaming. Didn't want to have no problems. Then I left my friends to take care of it and I went and got a milkshake 'cause it was real hot out and I needed to cool down. That made the papers too and there was a lotta panic in L.A. and I felt at peace.

STERLACE: Who decided to write on the walls in the victims' blood?

MANSON: That was me, with a little help from my friends. John and Paul and George had shown me the direction we should go. Pigs on the wall and Helter Skelter on the fridge. Wrapped everything up in a bright red ball. We were blackbirds singing in the dead of night only waiting for this moment to arise.

STERLACE: Did you ever feel guilt for what you had done?

MANSON: Not while I was alive but now it's getting to me a bit. Getting to me a lot. Changing here and it don't feel too good. Used to think you could only do what you did. There was no right or wrong. Now I see things differently. How would I have liked them doing it to me? Sure I wouldn't have liked it at all.

STERLACE: I'd like to get your feelings about other cult leaders.

MANSON: Interesting how those guys they're all kind of different and all kind of the same.

STERLACE: ...and all kind of insane.

MANSON: Just 'cause I can leap tall buildings in a single bound don't make me crazy. Minute you're a little different the shrinks are all over you trying to shrink you down to their size, to the size that society wants you to be, needs you to be. Those bastards don't know nothing about creativity. They don't like anyone going 'round exercising their personal freedom. Want to put you in a box and sail you out to sea. What is the sound of one hand smacking? Those pricks were always trying to get me not to think. But it's not illegal yet. Like to think all day sometimes till smoke is comin' out my ears. Maybe some of these doctors should learn how to think before they tell other folks how to. Drugs can help. Drugs can hurt. Like to open their throats and shove some Thorazine and Lithium down them. See how they like it.

STERLACE: Back to cult leaders.

MANSON: Said I was one, but never saw it myself. Saw myself as a sheep in wolf's clothing. The lord sent me to lieth down in green pastures with the children parents didn't want, didn't appreciate. Took them in, gave them pride, gave them discipline, gave them order, as much as you can have in all this chaos. Don't know if men walked on the moon. Couldn't see them from way down here.

STERLACE: Jim Jones.

MANSON: The electric Kool Aid acid test. You can drag a horse to water, and you can force his head into the water, and you can hold it there, see what happens. He might drink. He might drown. But chances are slim that he'll love you. There are always folks who want to follow, that ask to follow, that ask how can they follow. Wouldn't mind following myself but never found no one better than me. Wonder sometimes if there ever was.

STERLACE: Jim Jones.

MANSON: Might have taken it a little too far. What good are disciples if they're dead and why take yourself out, that's just giving up. If you're dead, you can't cause no trouble.

STERLACE: L. Ron Hubbard.

MANSON: Old El Ron was about money. wasn't about love. Wanted to make folks clear but I was always clear. Prison will do that for you. Not sure I was born on a planet 75,000 years ago. Spaced out but not that spaced out.

STERLACE: David Koresh.

MANSON: The Wacko from Waco. Burned too many bridges. Government took him out kind of like they took all of us out. Seemed a little confused.

STERLACE: The Pope.

MANSON: Well, he's the biggest cult leader of them all, ain't he? Got them Catholics bamboozled and bewildered. Claims he's got a personal relationship with God. But where's the proof?

STERLACE: Donald Trump.

MANSON: Kind of impressed by how he worked himself up from the top to become King of the World. Agree with him on a lot of things. Don't have that strong work ethic that I look for in a leader. Don't have any brains. But he's definitely my favorite TV program.

STERLACE: Mel Lyman.

MANSON: Put me in Coach. Ran his people like a goddamn football team. Like me, he's a musician and you know none of us can ever be trusted. Ol' Mel taught his folks that I made a statement, but he didn't say what kind.

STERLACE: Hitler.

MANSON: Met old Adolph down here. He told me he liked my work. At least that's what I think he said. He don't speak English too good.

STERLACE: Jesus.

MANSON: Only Jew from the Middle East with blonde hair and blue eyes. Don't suppose I'll ever get to talk to Him but I'll keep Him in my prayers.

STERLACE: Anthony Robbins.

MANSON: Unlimited power to con people. There's gotta to be more to life than him folks.

STERLACE: What did you think of the Unabomber?

MANSON: Had some good ideas but he was a bit cut off in the woods living alone in his little metal shack. That ain't no way to live. People need people. Sending letter bombs is so impersonal. I sent my representatives. No matter who you are, no matter what you're into you need people. Like they say in the ad, we're all connected.

STERLACE: Woody Allen? Do you think he's guilty?

MANSON: Well, he sure ain't innocent. You start taking your girlfriend's adopted daughter to the park and treating her like you're her father, pushing her on the swings, holding her hand so she doesn't walk into traffic then all of a sudden one day a few years later you say, I just happen to have this camera...I'd like to take a few snapshots of you, just take off your clothes and we'll create some art. You think that sounds like an innocent man? The devil, she'll straighten him out when he gets here.

STERLACE: What do you think about what Dylan said?

MANSON: What he say?

STERLACE: Not he, she, Dylan... Woody's daughter.

MANSON: Dylan is Woody's daughter? That don't make no sense.

STERLACE: Forget it, let's talk about you.

MANSON: Never saw myself as a cult leader. More of a teacher and a guide. More of a mystical magical magician spreading the Gospel of Charlie wherever I go. Look to me for the answers and you shall find.

STERLACE: Isn't it true that life has no meaning?

MANSON: Depends what you mean by that. Could be some meaning we don't know 'bout. That we'll never know 'bout. God might be a keeping it from us 'cause too much meaning might be a dangerous thing. If we knew the meaning of life we all might act different or we might not 'cause we could be programmed to do exactly what we've already been doing in which case I shouldn't be here 'cause it ain't my fault. On the other hand, there might be something called free will which means we're all doing what we want to do or what we need to do.

STERLACE: So, you think life might have meaning.

MANSON: It might. It might not. Why are you asking me?

STERLACE: Why am I asking you anything?

MANSON: Think you like to ask questions of wise men like me 'cause sometimes our answers can be illuminating. If there's no meaning to life it either takes the sting out of things 'cause who would get upset about things that don't mean anything or it means existence stings more 'cause it creates a sense of meaninglessness where you're floundering through life without real purpose heading quickly towards death which fortunately don't exist, at least not the way a lot of folks picture it. They think it might be nothin' but I am dying proof that ain't the case.

STERLACE: The Dalai Lama says it's important to be happy.

MANSON: Who would know better than him? Maybe you shouldn't be talking to me. Maybe you should be seeing about getting a sit down with the Lama or the Pope or Jesus himself. All could probably give you more satisfactory answers than I ever could. Not on their spiritual plane. Just a little boy trying to change the whole wide world. If you ask me enough times about the meaning of life or the infield fly rule or the holocaust or Noah's Ark I might come up with something good. But I'm out in the middle of the ocean paddling furiously and I might not make it back to shore. Do you know who you're talking to? Do you know who you're talking to? Let me tell you, you don't want to get on my bad side.

STERLACE: Implying that you have a good side.

MANSON: 'Course I got a good side. Just 'cause they don't talk about it, just 'cause you don't hear about it don't mean I don't have it. I'm a boy scout. I'm a choir boy. I can heal the lame and cure the sick. I can raise the dead and lift the roof. I can perform feats of strength and read your mind.

STERLACE: What am I thinking now?

MANSON: You're thinking when will this son of a bitch ever shut up. I'm evil and I'm good. I'm happy and I'm sad. No one is as great as me. No one is as bad. No one can see what I can see. No one can feel what I can feel. No one can know what I know, you know. I'm operating at near full capacity and you can't do no more than that. When I'm happy I'm fully happy. When I'm sad I'm fully sad.

STERLACE: Which are you right now?

MANSON: Fully happy because I'm sharing this moment with you and your never-ending series of stupid questions. Did you think of them all by yourself or did your Mommy and Daddy help you?

STERLACE: What's your purpose?

MANSON: I'm here and I was there to spread joy to the children, to teach them how to live and how to breathe. Any of them show up here I'll keep teaching them even though it might be a little too late. What more can I do than what I've done? What more can I give than what I've loved? Won't you listen to my song? Like to make love to the whole damn world but that would take a long, long time.

STERLACE: What's your definition of spirituality?

MANSON: It's the light inside of you and if you go deep down the well, you'll see it shining there. You can access it with your heart or your head, but it never burns out. It's the eternal flame of peace and forgiveness and where it goes no one knows.

STERLACE: Are you selfish?

MANSON: I'm the most selfish man who ever lived. I'm only out for me. I want to get what I can get, and I'll always take what I can take. Any man who tells you he's not out for himself is lying.

STERLACE: But teaching the children isn't selfish.

MANSON: 'Course it is. Teaching the children ain't nothing but selfish. Nothing makes me feel better than spreading the Gospel of Charlie, the nine commandments of Charlie. The meek won't inherent the earth. Only the strong will survive. If you're going to dance, dance. If you're going to swim, swim. You don't bring a knife to a gun fight. You bring a rifle.

STERLACE: Tell me a story.

MANSON: There once was a stupid, silly man who asked stupid, silly questions so I chopped him up like fire wood and stuffed him in a furnace.

STERLACE: Tell me a nice story.

MANSON: There once was a loving father who gave all he had to take care of his family. He worked hard every day of his life. But his family didn't care. Took advantage of his generosity. Little by little they crushed his spirit. So, he laid down and died.

STERLACE: I said a nice story.

MANSON: There once was a land of candy and cream where no one was crazy. Everybody was tall and healthy and glowing with the self-satisfaction of a life well led. They had no regrets and no fears. Is that what you want to hear? A fairytale that can never be? Why not face the truth? Does it scare you so much?

STERLACE: Yes.

MANSON: Well, I can't help you then. I am the truth and the way and if you follow me, I can show you things you need to be shown. But you're so afraid that instead of getting on your knees you're thinking too much when you shouldn't be thinking at all.

STERLACE: Not at all?

MANSON: Not one little bit.

STERLACE: Did you ever think about what you would have done with your life if you hadn't ended up being a psychotic murderous cult leader?

MANSON: Those are your labels, not mine. I'm a know-it-all fool with answers to all of the world's questions.

STERLACE: Like what?

MANSON: Like anything and everything.

STERLACE: That's so specific.

MANSON: If I wanted to I could write the world's greatest self-help manual. In it would be step by step instructions on the best ways to go about things. First off, your mother and father make love and from that seed you wind up in her womb. While there try to relax, you're stuck there for a little while and though you don't know it at the time you'll never have it so good again. You're floating in a misty haze and you're connected to the universe through your mother. Sometimes it's blissful, sometimes it's rocky but it's always the beginning of a magical adventure. Then one day you're let out into the world. Just go with it, don't fight it. There's no going back. You can only go forward into the light of oppression. Your mother will usually try to steer you as you go, but don't let her. Resist her with all your might. She might try to tell you how to wear your hair, what kind of friends to have, what kind of groups you should belong to. Resist. Always be your own man and whether you're five or fifty never ever care what people think about you. Stay true to your vision of yourself. Never let them sway you from your true path. If I hadn't been a leader type I might have enjoyed being a carpenter or a milk man or a vet. I might have been a butcher, a baker, or a candle stick maker. Most likely I would have taken my guitar to the subway or park and played my music for the people. Collected change in a cup. But I was made for bigger things. I was born to guide those who gone astray. Even in prison I tended over my flock from afar and they saw that it was good.

STERLACE: Did you have a Facebook page?

MANSON: Sure did. It's still active. Follow me on Facebook I always say. With all the hustle and bustle of the modern world it's the best way to keep in touch. Got full up real quick. Everybody wanted to be my friend and read my words. Like to inhabit folks' minds. That's why I'm talking to you. You're my new way to keep in touch.

STERLACE: So, you could say I'm a conduit for the Lord.

MANSON: You could say that and what's more you'd be right. If you have any other friends who'd like to get my word out, send them to me. Always looking to attract more followers. Always.

STERLACE: What do you look for in a follower?

MANSON: Prefer a young man or woman who ain't too bright, who's kind of insecure, who's searching for something to fill the hole.

STERLACE: Is there really a hole?

MANSON: 'Course not but it's good to let them think there is 'cause then you can fill it. Give me someone in need of guidance and I'll give you the man.

STERLACE: Is it lonely down here?

MANSON: Sometimes. It takes a little getting used to but me and Steve McQueen spent a lot of time in solitary and we're damn sure used to isolation.

STERLACE: What do you think about when you're alone?

MANSON: That maybe I'll never see anyone ever again. That maybe I'll be left to rot. But the longer I'm alone I find the less lonely I feel. There are seven levels of awareness and when you tap into all seven at once it can be a glorious thing to behold. You can daydream so much that it feels like night dreaming. Being awake is kind of limiting but being awake while dreaming you're sleeping, it don't get any better than that. Level one is your conscious mind worrying about the little things. Level two you start to get really paranoid with much justification. Level three your mind stretches out in a golden field. Level four you're lying on the side of the road while cars run you over. Level five you go backward and forward in time to a distorted past and a brutal future. Level six is a collage of sound and light flashing like a tiny million suns. Here the pain is exquisite.

STERLACE: ...And level seven?

MANSON: That's where you realize that plants can think but you still gotta eat them, that there is no easy way out, that you'll have to live this misery over and over till you get it right, that you'll never grow up no matter how old you grow, that you'll love and you'll hate sometimes at the same time, that your brain is a skyscraper without any elevators, that your mind is a train you can't jump off, that you'll never get out on parole, that you're part of the wall and it's part of you, that we got crazy old men sending young boys off to die, that all the dreams you had never mattered, that death is all or nothing at all.

STERLACE: Where would you go in a time machine?

MANSON: Probably go and follow Christ around. See if He was all He was cracked up to be. Did He really do all the things they say He did or was it all just a nice little story. Maybe I'd write the first Gospel. Now a reading from the Gospel according to Charlie. Then when I came back to the present I'd check to see if I was in the *Bible*. Or maybe I'd travel into the future, see what that's like. Careful not to go too far or you might miss the end of the world. Wouldn't mind seeing how screwed up everything's bound to get. You think it's bad now, you ain't seen nothing yet.

STERLACE: Did you ever think about getting a real job?

MANSON: What's real? Oh, like where you sell your time for a little money and the boss is on your back twenty-five hours a day and the customer is always right even if he's a fucking asshole. No thanks, I'll stick with prison.

STERLACE: Ever do much traveling?

103

MANSON: Nah, not much. Always too lazy to go traipsing around the country. Let the world come to me. What would I get out of going somewhere?

STERLACE: Meet some interesting people, see some interesting places.

MANSON: Been in reform school, been in jail, been in prison, been in cities, been in the desert. Met enough interesting people, seen enough interesting places.

STERLACE: Let's cover some of the crazy rumors about you.

MANSON: Like what?

STERLACE: That you auditioned for the Monkees.

MANSON: Yeah, heard 'bout how TV was looking for four young men who could sing so I made a daring escape from jail and went and stood in line with all the other losers. Needless to say, I didn't get it. Think they thought I was too far out.

STERLACE: It's been said that you were there when Bobby Kennedy got shot.

MANSON: Who do you think gave the order?

STERLACE: What did you think of Bono declaring that U2 were taking "Helter Skelter" back from you?

MANSON: I'm taking "Helter Skelter" back from them. That guy is a little too full of himself yet he's mighty insecure. While I was playing guitar alone rotting in my cell he was out there singing to millions and at the end of his concerts he'd ask the crowd to not forget about him. Never had that problem myself. No one has ever forgotten about me.

STERLACE: Have you ever listened to Marilyn Manson?

MANSON: No, never heard her.

STERLACE: He.

MANSON: Whatever. These people can take my name, but they'll never be me.

STERLACE: Does it excite you when people sing your songs?

MANSON: Don't mean much to me. Like singing them myself. I'm the only one who can do 'em right.

STERLACE: You don't have any opinions on what the Beach Boys did or Guns N' Roses?

MANSON: The Wilsons changed my words without telling me. Didn't appreciate that. Maybe I should have sent some girls to *their* houses.

STERLACE: What was it like when you lived with Dennis Wilson?

MANSON: Dennis let us all down.

STERLACE: Did you see that movie he made with James Taylor?

MANSON: Don't like James Taylor. Always thought I was better than him. Why did he get so much? Should have been me working with the Beatles or the Warner Brothers. You can't tell me he's a better singer than me, a better writer. Got fucked over by existence.

STERLACE: Did you know Dennis Hopper?

MANSON: Yeah, he was a motherfucker. Went with him to Vegas one weekend to see Elvis but we was so fucked up they threw us out. Never did get to see Elvis. No big deal. Maybe I'll catch him down here.

STERLACE: So, Elvis is here?

MANSON: 'Course. Weren't no choir boy.

STERLACE: What about Hopper? You talk to him lately?

MANSON: Yeah, a little. Not as much fun as he used to be. Now that's he's sober. You might want to talk to him. He never shuts up. Hard to get a word in edgewise.

STERLACE: You mean...

MANSON: I mean he never shuts up, like he talks right over you. All it is is me me me me me. Like no one else matters. Like no one else fucking matters. I like a good listener 'cause I got a lot of important things to say.

STERLACE: Such as?

MANSON: Don't put me on the spot.

STERLACE: It's been said that fear turns you on.

MANSON: Fear is a stone-cold tool for getting the weak minded to behave the way you want them to. All you gotta do is make them fearful. You do what I say or you ain't getting that promotion. You follow my instructions or I'll cut you right open. You give me what I want or I won't love you. Instill fear and you'll have them right where you want them. Folks don't like to be scared, don't like to be anxious. People were scared of me even though I was in prison, even though I was behind bars. What if Manson escapes, what if he comes to get us? What the fuck, man. What are the odds of that? Like I'm going to be coming down their chimney when I come. Jesus, if I ever could have escaped I would have been heading straight for the mountains and hiding for the rest of my natural life or would of put on a business suit and tried to blend in with the squares. Maybe sell life insurance door to door. Might you die someday? Might I be the one to kill you? If I was president I'd just go ahead and drop the bomb on a couple of our allies and you'd see how quick all the other countries would fall in line. When you rob a bank or a liquor store you don't say pretty please mister can I have all your money...you stick a gun in their face and threaten to blow them to kingdom come. Fear makes things happen. Fear gets things done. Used to use it all the time. Worked like a charm. Intimidating folks pays dividends. Even if they're just fearful of your disapproval. Always made sure that my wayward girls wanted my parental like approval. Was something they didn't care about with their father but they needed it from me. 'Course, sometimes you gotta go the opposite way. Was a little too much fear being shed by Sharon and the others so I made sure to reassure the LaBiancas that we wasn't going to hurt them. Sometimes you gotta make them only slightly fearful to get the job done. All depends on the situation. For instance, if you break into a house and you're trying to get somebody to open a safe for you then you only lather on a little fear 'cause otherwise they might forget the combination. It might fly right outta their head. You need to think things through. If charm works better than fear, then charm them. If a sledge hammer is called for use a sledge hammer. Drugs can help. You drug somebody up it's even easier to make them paranoid. You can put them on a trip and scare the bejesus out of them. You see how cats react when a stranger comes in their house. It's the same for people. Unless you surprise one of those second amendment nuts. They'll shoot you just as soon as look at you. They almost want you to break in. If there's anything I've learned it's that the strong survive and the weak fall into a hole and never get out. Wallflowers ain't gonna become powerful or rich or feared or famous or fulfilled. They're gonna stand with their backs to the action never getting what they want, always losing what they have and that includes their minds. Folks wear their histories on their back but it ain't happening now. Folks fear their future, get all anxious 'bout it but it ain't happening yet. Folks take freedom for granted but I never did. Folks think they ain't smart enough or good enough but Jesus Christ almost all of you are better than the goddamn president. If everybody was secure in their own skin, not worried at all 'bout what others thought of them it'd be a much better world. Sick to death of worry warts and pussies. Most of you haven't been in prison, haven't been thrown into hell, haven't been smacked around anywhere as much as you think you have. You're on a pleasure cruise compared to my life. I could wake you up but you won't listen. You never listen.

STERLACE: Does it strike you funny that they call them the Manson murders?

MANSON: Don't call it the Oswald assassination. Don't call it the Booth assassination. Guess I'm a little more important than Sharon and the others. Guess I'm a little more interesting. You're not talking to her, you're talking to me.

STERLACE: What do you think of *Once Upon A Time… In Hollywood*?

MANSON: Not much. Thought it was gonna be 'bout me. Shoulda been 'bout me. Stead it was 'bout two pretty boys. Lot of boring shit about acting and actors. Bruce Lee, man he don't have nothin' to do with me. Sharon Tate going to the movies what the hell is that. Shoulda shown me going to the movies. Anything with me is automatically more interesting. Hence this book, hence *Helter Skelter* on TV. Wasn't 'bout fucking Sharon Tate. Was about me. Why'd you think people watched it?

STERLACE: So, you think Tarantino should have utilized you more.

MANSON: 'Course. If'n he wanted a better picture. Gives me one or two fuckin lines. "Is Terry home? I'm a friend of his." Shit, that's pure genius. How did he ever come with up with that? Two and a half hour picture and I'm in it for two and a half seconds. Talk about wasting a golden opportunity. It's like if you came down here to talk to me and when you put out the book I was only on one page. Charlie, thanks for talking with us. I ain't got nothing better to do. The End.

STERLACE: What did you think of the actor that played you?

MANSON: He didn't have nothing to do in *Hollywood* but he was great as me in *Mindhunter*. Almost like looking in a mirror.

STERLACE: Did you see the scene Tarantino deleted?

MANSON: Yeah. Wasn't much there either but at least they let me talk a bit. In a two-and-a-half-hour movie they didn't have time for two and a half minutes of me? Must say though I never said the words Columbia Records and Tapes in my life...until now. Shit, if they had signed me to Columbia Records and Tapes we might be having a little different conversation right now. Charlie, tell me about your first number one. Charlie, your songs are so wonderful. Tell us all about them.

STERLACE: What about Steve Railsback in *Helter Skelter*?

MANSON: He was alright but he could have been a little better, a little more controlled. Guess it's hard to capture me 'cause I'm so special.

STERLACE: You think very highly of yourself.

MANSON: Someone has to.

STERLACE: What would your advice be for those suffering from lack of self-esteem?

MANSON: Now God made us all in His image and it stands to reason that since He's pretty goddamned good, you're pretty goddamned good. Have you made mistakes? Of course you have. That's part of life. But don't dwell on them. While billions of people around the world are ignoring you you've got the freedom to love yourself. Maybe things will get better right around the corner. Maybe you're a wonderful human being and no one has noticed yet. Sometimes happiness don't come from within. Get out there and do something. That's what I did. When everybody's talking 'bout you you'll know that you've arrived.

STERLACE: Why is there suffering?

MANSON: Must be part of God's great plan to keep us in line. He gave us free will and the way we use it causes suffering. I've suffered a lot. Society beat me down and locked me up. I had it bad. But did I complain? Hell yeah, I complained. Why was I being singled out? What had I done wrong? After crucifixion comes the resurrection.

Sometimes just when you think it can't get any worse, it gets better.

STERLACE: All we need is love.

MANSON: Sure. Love is what keeps us going when all around us is dark. Love your neighbor. Understand your neighbor. Walk out of the sand and into the light. Do what love tells you to do and I'll do what it tells me to do.

STERLACE: I can't help but think you would have been a great evangelist.

MANSON: Could have held them spellbound. Replace Billy Graham with me and you would have really had something. Standing up on a soapbox, raising my voice to the heavens, putting the fear of God into them. Pass the collection plate and give me all your money.

STERLACE: I can picture it.

MANSON: Dearly beloved, you are gathered here today to listen to your old friend Charlie. Yea, though I have walked through the valley of the shadow of death I shall fear no evil because I am the biggest bastard in the valley. I am the truth and the way and the life. Give me everything you can give and then give me some more. Listen to me you heathens and lowlifes. Listen to me you fornicating adulterers. It's not over till it's over. Repent and turn your life over to good old Charlie. I'm here for you. I'll always be here for you. Maybe I should start a congregation down here. Up to my neck in sinners. I say unto you, it's not too late to be saved or now that I think of it maybe it is. Jesus said to give up your possessions and follow him but he ain't here and I'm the closest thing around this Godforsaken hole so will I do?

STERLACE: Then again maybe you're not cut out for it.

MANSON: All I can do is be the best Charlie I can be.

STERLACE: Which isn't saying much.

MANSON: Actually, it's saying a lot. Don't see no one making a movie about you, writing books about you. It ain't delusions of grandeur if you ain't delusional. Take Trump. He thinks he's the greatest man who ever lived, the savior America's been waiting for. Well, maybe he is and maybe he ain't but he's sure as hell been vindicated about being the center of the universe. Everybody's paying attention to him, everybody's hanging on his every word. He feels he can do no wrong and maybe he can't. He never gets punished for his evil, that's for sure. Still, one day soon he'll be down here with me and I'm hoping I'll get a chance to straighten him out. He thinks the press is tough on him? He ain't seen nothing yet.